Read All About It!

A Kit Classic
Volume 1

by Valerie Tripp

★ American Girl®

Published by American Girl Publishing
Copyright © 2000, 2014 American Girl

Questions or comments? Call 1-800-845-0005,
visit **americangirl.com**, or write to Customer Service,
American Girl, 8400 Fairway Place, Middleton, WI 53562.

Printed in China
14 15 16 17 18 19 20 LEO 10 9 8 7 6 5 4 3 2 1

Cover image by Michael Dwornik and Juliana Kolesova

Cataloging-in-Publication Data available from the Library of Congress

Beforever

Beforever is about making connections.
It's about exploring the past, finding your
place in the present, and thinking about the
possibilities your future can bring. And it's about
seeing the common thread that ties girls from
all times together. The inspiring characters you
will meet stand up for what they care about
most: Helping others. Protecting the earth.
Overcoming injustice. Through their courageous
stories, discover how staying true to your own
beliefs will help make your world better
today—and tomorrow.

❧ TABLE *of* CONTENTS ❧

Good News

lick, clack, clackety!

Kit Kittredge smiled as she typed. She loved the sound the typewriter keys made as they struck the paper and the *ping!* of the bell when she got to the end of a line. She loved the inky smell of the typewriter ribbon, and the way the black letters looked as they marched across the page, telling a story the way *she* wanted it told.

It was a hot afternoon in August. Kit and her best friend Ruthie were in Kit's room writing a newspaper for Kit's dad. Kit was not a very good typist. She used only her two pointer fingers, and she made a lot of mistakes, which she had to xxxxx out. But Dad never minded. Every night when he came home from work, he gave Kit the real newspaper so that she could read the headlines and the baseball scores and the funnies.

He was always very pleased when Kit gave him one of her newspapers in return.

Kit finished the paragraph she was typing. "Read me what we have so far," said Ruthie.

Kit cleared her throat and read:

```
Ruthie Smithens and Kit Kittredge are
reading lots of books this summer.
Ruthie has read the Blue, Yellow, XXX
and Red Fairy Books by Andrew Lang.
She is nowt reading The Lilac Fairy
Book. "I am interested in princes
and princesses, so I like fairy tales,"
ssaid Ruthie. Kit Kittredge is rreading
The Adventures of Robin Hood and His
Merry Men. "I like the way Robin Hood
tricks the bad guy, the Sheriff of
Nottingham," said Kit." And the way he
robs rich people and gives their money
to poor people. I think it would bee
great to live in XXX Sherwood Forest."
```

"That's good," said Ruthie when Kit finished reading. "I like it."

"Me, too," said Kit. "What should we write about now?"

"Write about Charlie and the cookies," said Ruthie.

Charlie was Kit's brother, who was sixteen.

Kit thought a moment. Then she typed:

```
Congratulations to Charlie Kittredge!
He et set a World's Record today. He
ate A a Hole Xwhole plate of gingersnaps
that were supposed to be fore Mother's
garden club. Charlie is going to college
in a few weeks. He should try out for XX
the Eating Team!
```

Ruthie looked over Kit's shoulder and giggled as she read what Kit had written. "Now what?" she asked.

Kit picked up a pencil and put it behind her ear so that she'd look like a newspaper reporter. "Well," she said, "we could write about how hot it is."

Ruthie nodded, quickly at first, then slower and slower. Finally she let her chin fall to her chest, closed her eyes, and pretended to snore.

"You're right," said Kit. "Weather's boring. There aren't any *people* in it. This is supposed to be a newspaper, not a *snooze*paper."

"You could write about how your mother redecorated your room," Ruthie said. "I think it's as pretty as a princess's room, don't you?"

"Mmm," answered Kit, with a crooked smile. "It's okay. It's just a little too . . . *pink* for me. I'd rather sleep in a tree house, like Robin Hood."

Ruthie shook her head. "You're crazy," she said.

"Yup," said Kit cheerfully. She knew Ruthie was right, of course. Her room *was* pretty. Mother had redecorated it for her earlier that summer as a surprise. And, as with everything Mother did, it was lovely. Kit's room was painted pale pink with white trim. There was a canopy bed as high and white and fluffy as a cloud, and a dressing table with a lacy skirt around it. The desk was white and spindly-legged. It looked too delicate to hold the big black typewriter that crouched on it.

Mother had asked Kit to keep the typewriter in the closet, please, and take it out only when she used it. But Kit always forgot to put the typewriter away. Besides, she used it a lot. The typewriter ended up being on the desk all the time, even though it looked out of place in the frilly room.

Kit squirmed on the poufy stool that had replaced her old swivel chair. She believed in telling the truth straight-out. But so far she hadn't told Mother that she *felt* as out of place in the frilly room as the typewriter *looked.* Mother was so pleased with all the lacy pink-ness, and so sure the room was a girl's dream. *Which it probably is,* Kit admitted to herself, *just not mine.*

"The redecorating story's no good because Dad knows all about it," she said to Ruthie. "It's not new." Kit sighed. "I wish something would happen around here. Some dramatic *change.* Then we'd have a headline that would really grab Dad's attention."

"Like in the real newspapers," said Ruthie.

"Exactly!" said Kit.

"I don't know," said Ruthie. "When my parents read the headlines these days, they get worried. The news is always about the Depression and it's always bad. I don't think we want our paper to be like that."

"No," said Kit. "We want *good* news."

She knew there hadn't been much good news in the real newspapers for a long time. The whole country was in a mess because of the Depression. Dad had explained it to her. About three years ago, people got nervous about their money and stopped buying as many things as they used to, so some stores had to close down. The people who worked in the stores lost their jobs. Then the factories that made the things the stores used to sell had to close down, so the factory workers lost their jobs, too. Pretty soon the people who'd lost their jobs had no money to pay their doctors or house painters or music teachers, so those people got poorer, too.

Kit was glad that her dad still had his job at his car dealership. She and Ruthie knew kids at school whose fathers had lost their jobs. They'd seen those fathers selling apples on street corners, trying to earn a few cents a day. Some kids had disappeared from school because their families didn't have enough money to pay the rent anymore, and they had to move. Dad said the Depression was like a terrible slippery hole. Once you fell in, it was almost impossible to get out. Kit knew that the Depression was getting worse all the time because the newspaper headlines said so almost every night.

But inside Kit's house, no dramatic changes worth a headline seemed to be happening. The girls were about to give up on finding any news—good or bad—when Charlie popped his head in the door.

"Hey, girls," he said. "Mother's garden club's here. You better get downstairs quick if you want anything to eat. I saw Mrs. Culver already diving headfirst into the nut dish."

"Thanks for telling us, Charlie," said Kit.

"Oh, boy!" said Ruthie. "Maybe there'll be some cake for us!"

"Maybe there'll be some *news* for us!" said Kit. She grabbed her notepad and took the pencil from behind her ear. "Come on!"

Kit and Ruthie thundered down the stairs. They slowed their steps in the hallway so that they wouldn't sound, as Mother always said, like a herd of stampeding elephants. Mother liked things to be *just so* when the garden club ladies came. She brought out all her best crystal, china, silver, and linen and arranged her most beautiful plants on the terrace where the ladies met. Kit could hear the ladies' voices and the clink of their iced tea glasses out on the terrace now.

Above all the other voices, Kit heard Mrs. Wolf complimenting Mother. "Margaret," Mrs. Wolf was saying, "your sponge cake is perfection. Mine is just that—a sponge!" Mrs. Wolf hooted at her own joke before she went on. "Please give me your recipe."

"I'd be glad to," said Mother, just as Kit and Ruthie stepped onto the terrace. Mother looked as cool and slender as a mint leaf in her pale green dress. Kit

wanted to fling herself at Mother and hug her. But she
held herself back. Her fingers had typewriter ink on
them. It would never do to leave ink stains on Mother's
perfect green dress!

Mother smiled when she saw the girls. Then she
turned to her guests and said, "Ladies, you remember
Ruth Ann Smithens and my daughter Kit, don't you?"

"Yes, of course!" said the ladies. "Hello, girls!"

"Hello," said Kit and Ruthie politely.

"Do help yourselves to some refreshments, girls,"
said Mother.

"We will!" said Kit and Ruthie, smiling broadly.

The girls filled their plates and retreated to a corner
behind a potted palm to enjoy their feast and observe
the ladies. At first the ladies discussed garden club
business, such as how to get rid of bugs, slugs, and
other garden pests. It was pretty boring, although the
girls did get giggly when Mrs. Willmore said she was
just beside herself because she had spots on her phlox.

Then the talk moved on to who was going to weed
the flower bed at the hospital, which the garden club
ladies took turns doing.

"I believe it is my turn," said Mrs. Howard. "But I'm

afraid I won't be able to weed this month. In fact ... "
She hesitated, and blinked her big round eyes. "I'm
afraid I won't be able to be part of the garden club at all
anymore."

Kit and Ruthie looked at each other and raised their
eyebrows. This sounded interesting. Why would Mrs.
Howard be quitting the garden club? Kit leaned forward so that she could hear better. *There may be a story
in this for our newspaper*, she thought.

All the ladies murmured that they were sorry, and
Mother said, "Oh, Louise! That's too bad!"

"Well," said Mrs. Howard, "I'm moving to Chicago.
My husband is already there, and so my son Stirling
and I are going to join him. He's pursuing a business
opportunity."

"Ahh!" said all the ladies brightly. They all knew
what that meant. Kit did, too. It meant that Mr. Howard
had gone to Chicago to look for a job. Everyone knew
that Mr. Howard had not had a job for two years, ever
since the company he worked for here in Cincinnati
had gone out of business.

"Where will you live in Chicago?" a lady asked.

"I'm not sure yet," said Mrs. Howard, blinking

again. "Mr. Howard hasn't settled anywhere. We'll be hither, thither, and yon for a while!"

The ladies smiled, but Kit saw little lines of concern on their faces. The whole thing sounded pretty fishy to Kit. *If the Howards have no place to live in Chicago, why are they leaving their house in Cincinnati?* she wondered. Then suddenly, it dawned on her. The Howards *couldn't* stay in their house. They didn't have enough money anymore. And Mr. Howard didn't have a job or a place for them to live in Chicago, either. That was the truth— Kit was sure of it. She was pretty sure that all the ladies knew it, too, but no one would say it out loud.

There was an awkward silence. Then Mother spoke up and made everything better. "I have a marvelous idea, Louise!" she said to Mrs. Howard. "We'd love it if you and dear Stirling would stay in our guest room until your husband is settled in Chicago and sends for you. Stirling is about Kit's age. I'm sure they'll get along beautifully."

Ruthie nudged Kit, but Kit held her finger to her lips to signal Ruthie not to say anything.

The ladies turned toward Mrs. Howard, waiting anxiously for her answer to Mother's invitation.

"Well," said Mrs. Howard slowly. "If you're *sure* it isn't too much trouble, Stirling and I would love to stay. Thank you, Margaret."

"That's all settled, then," said Mother calmly.

All the ladies brightened up, as if a cloud had blown away. Kit started scribbling notes on her notepad, and Ruthie whispered to her, "Who's this boy Stirling?"

Kit shrugged. "He's Mrs. Howard's son, I guess," she said. "I haven't met him."

"You will," said Ruthie. "He's going to be living in your house."

"Looks like it," said Kit. She liked the idea. Boys were always up to *something*. Stirling was sure to be a good source of stories for her newspaper for Dad. And it would be nice to have a boy around, especially after Charlie left for college. She and Stirling could play catch together. They could talk about the Cincinnati Reds baseball team, which Kit loved and Ruthie, quite frankly, didn't care about. And Stirling could join in when she and Ruthie acted out stories from the books they read.

Kit grinned at Ruthie. "When we play Robin Hood, Stirling can be the Sheriff of Nottingham," she said.

"Boys like to be the bad guy."

Ruthie had a big bite of cake in her mouth. She swallowed, then grinned back at Kit. "Well," she said. "You never know. Stirling might rather be Prince Charming and perform good deeds."

"He's already done one good deed," said Kit.

"What?" asked Ruthie.

"Come on," said Kit. "I'll show you."

The two girls slipped back inside the house and ran up the stairs to Kit's room. Kit stood in front of the typewriter. "Stirling's given us a headline," she said to Ruthie. "Look."

Kit typed in capital letters:

```
THE HOWARDS ARE COMING!
```

Read All About It

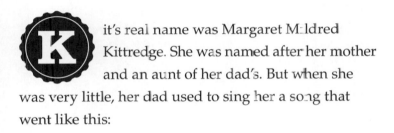 it's real name was Margaret Mildred Kittredge. She was named after her mother and an aunt of her dad's. But when she was very little, her dad used to sing her a song that went like this:

> *Pack up your troubles in your old kit bag*
> *and smile, boys, smile . . .*

It was a song he'd learned when he was a soldier fighting in the Great War. Kit loved it. She'd beg Dad, "Sing my song! Sing the kit song!" Pretty soon everyone began to call her Kit, which was also short for Kittredge, and the name stuck. Kit didn't like the name Margaret Mildred anyway. It didn't fit her. It was too flouncy. Kit was *not* a flouncy girl.

Right now she was feeling especially exasperated with flounces, because the stool she was sitting on was covered with them. Ruthie and the garden club ladies had left, and Kit was finishing her newspaper for Dad. She had to sit with one leg bent under her to reach the typewriter because the new flouncy stool was as soft as a marshmallow and too low.

Kit rolled her newspaper out of the typewriter and read it. She was very pleased with her headline, "The Howards Are Coming!"

That ought to get Dad's attention! Under the headline, Kit had written:

```
     Mrs. Howard is in Mother's garden club.
Mrs. Howard and her XXX son Stirling are
going to be staying with the Kittredge
family for a wwhile. Mr. Howard is in
Chicago. Having the Howards Here will be
Fun because Stirling can play catch with
Kit Kittredge, thr best nine-year-old
catcher in Cincinnati!!

                    Garden Club Trouble:
                    Phlox spots put Mrs.
                    Willmore beside herself!
```

Kit was struggling with her drawing of two Mrs.
Willmores when she heard the car horn's cheery *honk-honk* that signaled her favorite moment of the day. Dad
was home from work! Kit snatched up her newspaper,
flew downstairs, and burst out the door.

"Extra! Extra! Read all about it!" she shouted, waving her newspaper as Dad climbed out of his car.

Dad caught Kit up in his arms. "How's my girl?" he
asked.

"Great!" said Kit when her feet were back on the
ground. "Look! I've got a newspaper for you today!"

"Oh ho," said Dad. His blue eyes were twinkly. He
smiled a broad smile as he took Kit's newspaper and
handed her the real one. He read Kit's headline in a
booming voice. "'The Howards Are Coming!'" Then he
glanced at Kit and spoke in his normal voice. "Are they
coming for dinner?"

"Nope!" said Kit. "It's better than that! Read the
whole story!"

Kit watched as Dad's eyes scanned the story. She
noticed, much to her surprise, that his smile faded as
he read.

When Dad spoke his voice sounded funny, as if

he was trying too hard to be hearty. "Well," he said. "This *is* big news!" He gave Kit's hair a gentle tug. "I'm a lucky guy to have my own personal reporter to keep me on top of all the late-breaking stories," he said. "Come on, sweetheart. Let's go get the details from your mother."

Grownups are funny, Kit thought as she walked along next to Dad. *They don't react the way you expect them to.* Anyone would think that Dad was not pleased to have the Howards coming to stay. But why on earth wouldn't he be?

❀

Two days later, Kit and Ruthie were sitting on the front steps waiting for Stirling and Mrs. Howard to arrive. The girls were reading while they waited. At least, Ruthie was reading. Kit was too distracted. She was really just looking at the pictures in her book.

Kit's copy of *Robin Hood and His Adventures* had belonged to Charlie when he was her age. It had wonderful illustrations, which Kit loved to study. She especially loved reading about the tree houses that Robin and his men lived in. The houses were connected by swinging bridges and catwalks made out of vines. Kit longed to sleep in a tree house high up near the sky, surrounded by leaves. She imagined that at night, stars peeked through the leaves and the wind made the branches sway.

Kit had spent many hours drawing plans for a tree house that she and Ruthie could build. Kit was not very good at sketching. Her drawings always looked like doghouses stuck up in trees. They didn't look anything like the tree houses in Sherwood Forest.

"I bet," said Kit, "that Stirling can help us build a tree house."

"Mmm," said Ruthie, with the tiniest hint of irritation at being interrupted when she was deep into the story of *Beauty and the Beast.*

It was hot, and the girls were licking chunks of ice that had been chipped off the big block of ice in the icebox. Kit had her catcher's mitt next to her, too. She wanted Stirling to see right away that she was interested in books and baseball and was not the type of girl who only cared about things like dusting and baking and dresses.

Kit's ice chunk had melted to a sliver when, at last,

a cab pulled up to the end of the driveway. Kit and
Ruthie stood up and waited politely on the front steps.
The cab door opened, and Mrs. Howard and a boy got
out. When she saw Stirling, Kit felt as if someone had
dropped her ice chip down her back, she was so surprised.

Ruthie whistled softly. "I thought your mother said
that Stirling was about our age," she whispered. "He
looks like he's in kindergarten!"

Stirling stood next to the cab on two of the skinni-
est legs Kit had ever seen. He was short and pale and
skinny all over. His head looked too big for his scrawny
neck.

The screen door opened, and Mother came out of
the house. She stood between Kit and Ruthie and put
her hands on their shoulders.

"Mother!" whispered Kit indignantly. "Stirling's a
shrimp!"

"Now, Kit," said Mother. "Stirling is small for his
age because his health is delicate. But I'm sure he's
a very pleasant fellow." Gently, she pushed the girls
forward. "Come along, ladies," she said. "Let's go greet
our guests and make them feel welcome."

Kit and Ruthie and Mother walked down the steps
and toward the driveway. Mrs. Howard and the cab
driver were unloading boxes and suitcases from the
cab. Stirling just stood there.

"Oh!" said Mrs. Howard, all aflutter. "Margaret!
You are such a dear to have us!" She turned to Stirling.
"Shake hands with Mrs. Kittredge, lamby," she said.
"And say hello to Kit and Ruthie."

Stirling shook Mother's hand and nodded at the
girls. He looked even worse close-up. He had colorless
hair, colorless eyes, and a red, runny nose. Kit towered
over him, and Ruthie could have made two of him, he
was so puny.

"Oh, dear!" fussed Mrs. Howard. "All this excitement is not good for Stirling, the poor lamb! He'll have
to lie down right away and rest."

"Of course," said Mother. "Come with me and we'll
get him settled."

Kit and Ruthie stood on the driveway and watched
as Mrs. Howard and Mother propelled Stirling into
the house. The cab driver followed them, carrying an
armload of suitcases and boxes.

As soon as they were gone, Kit turned to Ruthie

and imitated Stirling. She snuffled her nose and made her eyes wide and unblinking.

Ruthie giggled, and then she said, "Of course in fairy tales you always learn not to judge by appearances. Lots of times perfectly nice people are under a spell. Think of *Beauty and the Beast*."

But over the next few days, it was clear to Kit that Ruthie's *Beauty and the Beast* theory didn't work in real life, at least not in Stirling's case. He never said a word. But then, he didn't have to. His mother did all the talking, and most of her sentences began with the words "Stirling can't."

When Kit and Ruthie invited Stirling to run through the sprinkler with them, Mrs. Howard said, "Stirling can't be in the sun because his skin is so fair. And Stirling can't run because he has weak lungs. Stirling can't get wet because he might catch a chill. And Stirling can't play in the yard because he's allergic to bee stings." Kit abandoned any idea of Stirling helping with a tree house or playing catch. Pretty soon, Kit and Ruthie gave up on inviting Stirling to do *anything*, because the answer was always "Stirling can't."

At first, Kit thought Mrs. Howard was making

the whole thing up about how fragile Stirling was. It
wasn't as if he had a sickness like rickets or scurvy or
any of the really interesting diseases Kit knew about
from reading pirate stories. Stirling didn't even have
any spots or rashes. However, after he'd been there a
week, Stirling got truly sick. Though it was only a cold,
he did have a fever and a terrible cough. Mrs. Howard
said that he had to stay in bed and have all his meals
brought to him on a tray.

Kit could hear Stirling coughing and sniffling and
blowing his nose all day long. Everyone had to tiptoe
past the door to his room so they wouldn't disturb
Stirling in case he was napping. Kit held her nose
when she passed by, because the hall outside his room
smelled strongly of Vicks VapoRub even though the
door was always shut.

But one afternoon, Kit noticed that the door to the
guest room was open. She sneaked a peek inside. Stirling was propped up on the pillows, and Mrs. Howard
was nowhere to be seen. Of course, it was hard to see
anything in the room. It was dark because the shades
were pulled down.

Kit stood in the doorway and looked at Stirling's

moon-white face on the pillow. "Gosh, it sure is stuffy in here," Kit said to Stirling. "Don't you want me to open the window or something?"

Stirling nodded.

Kit opened the window a crack so that a breath of air and a thin line of sunlight came through. "That's better!" she said. Kit turned to go. She was halfway to the door when she saw a photograph next to Stirling's bed that stopped her in her tracks. "Hey!" she said. "Is that Ernie Lombardi, the catcher for the Reds?"

Stirling's round eyes were as unblinking as an owl's as he looked at Kit. His nose was stuffed up, so his voice sounded weirdly low and husky. "Schnozz," he croaked.

For a second, Kit didn't understand. Then she laughed and nodded. "Schnozz!" she said. "That's Ernie Lombardi's nickname because he has such a big nose."

In answer, Stirling blew *his* nose, which made a nice honking sound.

Kit laughed again. "Ernie Lombardi is my favorite player on the Cincinnati Reds," she said. "He's the reason I'm a catcher. Well, and because my dad was a star catcher on his college team. Did you know that Ernie's the biggest guy on the Reds?"

"Six foot three," whispered Stirling hoarsely. "Two hundred and thirty pounds."

"Right!" said Kit, delighted. She rattled on. "It's funny that you like him," she said, "because he's so big and you're so little."

"That's why," said Stirling simply. He didn't sound the least bit offended, even though right after she spoke, Kit realized that she'd said something she shouldn't have.

"You know what?" said Kit, suddenly inspired. "I have a newspaper article about Ernie Lombardi. It has a photograph of him holding seven baseballs in one hand at the same time. It used to be tacked up on my wall. My mother wouldn't let me put it back up after my room was painted pink, but I bet I can find it. Want to see it?"

Stirling nodded vigorously, and Kit noticed that his eyes weren't colorless at all. They were gray.

"Okay!" she said. "I'll get the article and you can read all about it!" Kit tore back to her room and rummaged through the drawers of her desk. Where was

that newspaper article with the photo of Schnozz?
She hoped Mother hadn't thrown it away! Scrambling
wildly through the bottom drawer, Kit found the scrap
of newspaper at last. She raced back to Stirling's room
shouting, "I found it!"

Kit flung open the door and *BAM!* The door hit
Mrs. Howard, who was standing right inside with a
silver tray in her hands.

"MY LAND!" shrieked Mrs. Howard. She lurched
forward and the tray, which had one of Mother's best
china teacups and saucers on it, went flying. The hot
tea sloshed out all over the rug. The cup hit the floor
and shattered, and the tray clanged to the ground with
a noise like cymbals.

"Oh dear, oh *dear!*" fussed Mrs. Howard. At the
same time, Stirling started to cough loudly. Kit tried to
apologize in a voice louder than his coughs, and Charlie appeared and added to the commotion by asking,
"What happened? What's all the noise?"

They were all talking at once when Mother came in.
"Good gracious!" she said above all the racket. "*Now*
what?"

Everyone stopped talking, even Mrs. Howard.

"Will someone please tell me what is going on?" asked Mother, not sounding at all like her usual serene self.

Everyone looked at Kit.

Kit knew that Mother disliked messes, so she tried to explain how this one was just an accident. "I was coming in here to show Stirling my picture of Ernie Lombardi," she said, "and I didn't know that Mrs. Howard was right behind the door. I was in a hurry and I—"

Mother held up her hand to stop Kit. "Don't tell me," she said. "I can imagine the rest." She shook her head. "How many times have I told you to slow down and watch where you're going, Kit?"

"I'm sorry," said Kit.

Mother stooped down to pick up the broken cup. "Just look at what you've done," she said.

Kit was shocked. It wasn't like Mother to scold her like this. "But it wasn't *my* fault," she protested. "It was an accident. It was *nobody's* fault."

"Nobody's fault," repeated Mother. "And yet look at the mess we are in." She looked up at Kit. "Please go now," she said. "I'll help Mrs. Howard clean up. And

Kit, dear, please don't barge in here bothering Stirling and making messes anymore."

"But I didn't—" Kit began.

"That's enough, Kit," said Mother. "Go now."

Kit gave up. She turned on her heel and stormed back to her room. Mother seemed to think that the mess was all her fault, but it *wasn't*! She didn't *mean* to knock into Mrs. Howard. Stupid old Stirling was more to blame for the mess than Kit was. If he weren't sick, his mother wouldn't have been bringing him hot tea in the middle of the afternoon in the first place!

Kit flung herself down at the desk and looked at the wrinkled newspaper article in her hand. What did it matter that her photo of Ernie Lombardi holding seven baseballs was all crumpled up? She couldn't put it up on her new pink walls, and she sure wasn't going to show it to Stirling. She wasn't going to try to be nice to old sniffle-nose Stirling ever again. Look at the trouble it caused her.

Nothing made Kit more angry than being unjustly accused. She didn't mind a good fair fight. But to be blamed for something that was not her fault? That she could not stand. In books when people were accused of

crimes they didn't commit, someone like Nancy Drew
or Dick Tracy always came around and proved that
they were innocent. Kit could see that in her case, she
was going to have to speak for herself. She knew just
how to do it, too. She'd write a special newspaper for
Dad. Then at least *one* person would know her side of
the story.

Kit rolled a piece of paper into the typewriter. In
capital letters, she typed her headline:

IT'S NOT FAIR!

It's Not Fair

🌺 CHAPTER 3 🌺

Pounding the typewriter keys as hard as she could made Kit feel better. The good thing about writing was that she got to tell the whole story without anyone interrupting or contradicting her. Kit was pleased with her article when it was finished. It explained exactly what had happened and how the teacup was broken. Then at the end it said:

```
Sometimes a person is trying to do
something nice for another person and
it turns ᴋᴋᴋ out sadly badly by mistake.
When ssomething bad happens and it isn't
my anyone's fault, no one should be
blamed. It's not fair!
```

Kit pulled her article out of the typewriter and marched outside to sit on the steps and wait for Dad to

🌺 28 🌺

come home. She brought her book about Robin Hood to read while she waited.

She had not been reading long before the screen door squeaked open and slammed shut behind her. Kit didn't even lift her eyes off the page.

Charlie sat next to her. "Hi," he said.

Kit didn't answer. She was a little put out with Charlie for adding to the trouble in Stirling's room.

"What's eating you, Squirt?" Charlie asked.

"Nothing," said Kit as huffily as she could.

Charlie looked at the piece of paper next to Kit. "Is that one of your newspapers for Dad?" he asked.

"Yup," said Kit.

Charlie picked up Kit's newspaper and looked at the headline. "'It's Not Fair,'" he read aloud. Then he asked, "What's this all about?"

"It's about how it's wrong to blame people for things that are not their fault," said Kit. "For example, *me*, for the mess this afternoon."

"Aw, come on, Kit," said Charlie. "That's nothing. You shouldn't make such a big deal of it."

"That's easy for *you* to say!" she said.

Charlie took a deep breath in and then let it out.

"Listen, Kit," he said, in a voice that was suddenly serious, "I wouldn't bother Dad with this newspaper today if I were you."

Kit slammed her book shut and looked sideways at Charlie. "And why not?" she asked.

Charlie glanced over his shoulder to be sure that no one except Kit would hear him. "You know how lots of people have lost their jobs because of the Depression, don't you?" he asked.

"Sure," said Kit. "Like Mr. Howard."

"Well," said Charlie, "yesterday Dad told Mother and me that he's closing down his car dealership and going out of business."

"*What*?" said Kit. She was horrified. "But . . ." she sputtered. "But *why*?"

"Why do you think?" said Charlie. "Because nobody has money to buy a car anymore. They haven't for a long time now."

"Well, how come Dad didn't say anything before this?" Kit asked.

"He didn't want us to worry," said Charlie. "And he kept hoping things would get better if he just hung on. He didn't even fire any of his salesmen. He used his own savings to keep paying their salaries."

"What's Dad going to do now?" asked Kit.

"I don't know," said Charlie. "He even has to give back his own car. He can't afford it anymore. I guess he'll look for another job, though that's pretty hopeless these days."

Kit was sure that Charlie was wrong. "Anyone can see that Dad's smart and hardworking!" she said. "And he has so many friends! People still remember him from when he was a baseball star in college. Plenty of people will be glad to hire him!"

Charlie shrugged. "There just aren't any jobs to be had. Why do you think people are going away?"

"Dad's not going to leave like Mr. Howard did!" said Kit, struck by that terrible thought. Then she was struck by another terrible thought. "We're not going to lose our house like the Howards, are we?"

"I don't know," said Charlie again.

Kit could hardly breathe.

"It'll be a struggle to keep it," said Charlie. "Dad told me that he and Mother don't own the house completely. They borrowed money from the bank to buy it, and they have to pay the bank back a little every month. It's called a mortgage. If they don't have enough money to pay the mortgage, the bank can take the house back."

"Well, the people at the bank won't just kick us out onto the street, will they?" asked Kit.

"Yes," said Charlie. "That's exactly what they'll do. You've seen those pictures in the newspapers of whole families and all their belongings out on the street with nowhere to go."

"That is not going to happen to us," said Kit fiercely. "It's *not.*"

"I hope not," said Charlie.

"Listen," said Kit. "How come Dad told Mother and *you* about losing his job, but not *me*?"

Charlie sighed a huge, sad sigh. "Dad told me," he said slowly, "because it means that I won't be able to go to college."

"Oh, Charlie!" wailed Kit, full of sympathy and misery. She knew that Charlie had been looking forward to college so much! And now he couldn't go. "That's terrible! That's awful! It's not *fair.*"

Charlie grinned a cheerless grin and tapped one finger on Kit's newspaper. "That's your headline, isn't it?" he said. "These days a lot of things happen that aren't fair. There's no one to blame, and there's nothing that can be done about it." Charlie's voice sounded tired, as if he'd grown old all of a sudden. "You better get used to it, Kit. Life's not like books. There's no bad guy, and sometimes there's no happily ever after, either."

At that moment, Kit felt an odd sensation. Things were happening so fast! It was as if a match had been struck inside her and a little flame was lit, burning like anger, flickering like fear. "Charlie," she asked. "What's going to happen to us?"

"I don't know," said Charlie. He stood up to go.

"Wait," said Kit. "How come you told me about Dad? Was it just to stop me from bothering Dad with my newspaper?"

"No," said Charlie. "No. I told you because . . ." He paused. "Because you're part of this family, and I figured you deserve to know."

"Thanks, Charlie," said Kit. She was grateful to Charlie for treating her like a grownup. "I'm glad you told me," she said, "even though I wish none of it were true."

"Me, too," said Charlie. "Me, too."

After Charlie left, Kit sat on the step thinking. No wonder Dad had not been happy about the Howards coming to stay. He must have been worried about more mouths to feed. And no wonder Mother had been short-tempered today. When she said that even though it was nobody's fault, they were still in a mess, she must have been thinking of Dad. It wasn't his fault that they'd fallen into the terrible, slippery hole of the Depression, and yet, and yet . . . it surely seemed as though they had. Just like the Howards. Just like the kids at school. Just like the people she'd read about in the newspaper.

❀

The sun was setting, but it was still very hot outside. The air was so humid, the whole world looked blurry. Then, all too clearly, Kit saw a terrible sight. It was Dad. He was walking home. He did not see Kit yet, but she could see that he looked hot and tired. There was a discouraged droop to his shoulders that Kit had never seen before. It made Kit's heart twist with sorrow. For just the tiniest second, she did not want to face Dad.

She knew that when she did, she'd have to face the truth of all that Charlie had told her. But then Kit stood up and straightened her shoulders. Everything else in the whole world might change for Dad, but she wouldn't.

Kit ran to Dad the way she had done every other night of her life when he came home. Dad caught her up and swung her around.

When he put her down, Kit looked Dad straight in the eye. "Charlie told me," she said. "Is it true?"

Dad knelt down so that his eyes were level with Kit's. "Yes," he said. "It is."

"Are we going to be all right?" Kit asked.

"I don't know," said Dad. "I truly don't know."

Kit threw her arms around Dad and hugged him hard. She crumpled up her newspaper in her fist behind Dad's back. Her complaints about Stirling and the teacup seemed silly and babyish now. Charlie was right. Dad didn't need to read her newspaper. Dad knew all about trying to be nice to people and having it turn out badly. He knew all about having bad things happen that were nobody's fault. He knew all about things that were not fair.

❉

Kit was a practical girl. She thought it was a waste of time to worry about a problem when you could be *doing* something to solve it. But her family had never had a problem as serious as this one before. All night long Kit lay awake thinking, listening to Stirling cough—and worrying.

The night was very hot. Kit kicked her sheet off and turned her pillow over time and time again because it got sweaty so fast. Finally, Kit got up.

It always made her feel better to write. She took her notepad and a pencil out of her desk and sat at the window in the moonlight. She decided to make a list of all the ways she could save the family some money.

> *No dancing lessons*
> *No fancy dresses for dancing lessons*

Kit looked at her list and scolded herself. It was all very well to give up dancing lessons and fancy dresses. Those were things she didn't want. But how about things she *did* want?

With a soft sigh, Kit looked out the window. Then, sadly, she added to her list.

No lumber for a tree house
No new books
No tickets to baseball games
No sweets

There! thought Kit. *I'll show Dad my list tomorrow.*

But by the time Kit went downstairs to breakfast the next morning, Dad had already left.

"He's gone to meet a business friend," said Mother.

"It'd be great if his friend offered Dad a job, wouldn't it?" said Kit.

"Yes," said Mother. "It would." She smiled, but it wasn't one of her *real* smiles.

Kit felt all restless and jumpy. She wanted to be alone so that she could think and work on her list some more. She wandered around the yard for a while before she found a good hideaway under the back porch. *No one will find me here,* she thought.

But she had not been hidden long before Ruthie crawled in next to her.

"How do you always find me?" asked Kit.

Ruthie shrugged. "It's easy," she said. "I just think where I'd be if I were you, and that's where you are.

Why are you hiding, by the way?"

"My dad lost his job," said Kit.

"Oh," said Ruthie softly. "That's too bad. I'm sorry." The girls sat together in silence for a minute. That was a good thing about Ruthie. She'd sit and think with Kit. She didn't need to talk all the time. "What are you going to do?" Ruthie asked at last.

Kit handed Ruthie her list. "These are ways I can help save money," she said.

Ruthie read the list. "These are good," she said. "These'll help." But her voice sounded doubtful.

Kit sighed. "The truth is, I've just never given money much thought before," she said.

"I know," said Ruthie. "Me neither."

Kit understood that when Dad sold a car, people gave him money. Dad gave some of the money to Mother. She used it to buy food and clothes and to pay the electric bill and the iceman and to get things for the house. Once a month, Dad paid the bank twenty dollars, which, as Charlie had explained, was part of the money that Dad and Mother owed the bank because they'd borrowed it when they bought the house. If there was any money left over after everything was paid,

Dad put it in his savings account at the bank.

"Without Dad's job," said Kit to Ruthie, "there won't be any more money coming in. And Charlie said that Dad used up most of his savings to pay his salesmen as long as he could, so soon there won't be any money left in his savings. What'll we do then?"

"I've read lots of books about people who have no money," said Ruthie.

"Me, too," said Kit. "But most of them lived in the olden days on farms or in a forest where they could at least get nuts and berries. We live in modern times in Cincinnati. How will we get food when our money is gone? Will we move to a farm?"

"I don't think your mother would like that," said Ruthie.

"No," sighed Kit. "Besides, none of us knows any-thing about farming."

Ruthie scratched her knee. "I think," she said slowly, "we're going to have to hope that your dad gets another job."

"Yup," said Kit. "Maybe today." She looked at Ruthie. "What a great headline *that* would be!"

Mother's Brainstorm

❈ CHAPTER 4 ❈

But Dad didn't get a job that day, or the day after that, or the day after that, though he certainly seemed to be trying. Every day he put on a good suit and rode the streetcar downtown. Every day he said he was going to have lunch with a friend or a business acquaintance. Every day, Kit hoped he'd come home with the good news of a new job. But every afternoon, Dad came home tired and discouraged. All the bad news in the newspapers seemed to be about Kit's own life now.

One afternoon after a week had passed, Kit and Mother were on the back porch shelling peas when a huge black car pulled up in the driveway.

"Oh, no," sighed Mother.

Kit asked, "Is it Uncle Hendrick?"

Mother nodded. She took off her apron and handed

it and the peas to Kit. "Quick," she said. "Take these into the kitchen. And Kit, dear, while you're in there, pour us some iced tea and bring it to the terrace." Mother smoothed her hair, adjusted her smile, and walked gracefully toward the car.

Kit was glad to escape inside. Uncle Hendrick was her mother's uncle and the oldest relative Mother had left. He was tall and gray, and he lived in a tall, gray house near downtown Cincinnati. He always seemed to be in a bad mood, like Grandfather in the *Heidi* book before Heidi made him nice. *The last thing Uncle Hendrick needs is lemon,* Kit thought as she put a slice in his glass. *He's already a sourpuss.*

Kit put the iced tea on a tray and carried it to the terrace. Mother was sitting on a wicker chair, but Uncle Hendrick was pacing back and forth. When he saw Kit, he stopped.

Here it comes, thought Kit.

Without even saying hello, Uncle Hendrick barked at Kit, "What's the capital of North Dakota?"

"Bismarck," answered Kit. She was used to such questions from Uncle Hendrick. If he wasn't asking her about capitals, he was asking her multiplication facts. Worst of all were his word problems. "I have two bushels of Brussels sprouts I'm selling for five cents a peck," he said now. "How much do you pay me?"

Kit put the tray on the table to gain some time. She could never keep bushels and pecks straight. *And who wants two bushels of Brussels sprouts anyway?* she thought. "Um, fifty cents?" she guessed.

"Wrong!" said Uncle Hendrick. "You may go."

Mother gave Kit a sympathetic look. But Kit felt sorrier for Mother than she did for herself. She went inside, but she stayed in the dining room where she could hear everything they said.

"Margaret," Uncle Hendrick sighed. "Didn't I tell you and Jack what a mistake it was to sink all your money into that car dealership? If you two had listened to me, you would not be in the fix you are in now. And don't expect me to help you. I won't throw good money after bad."

"We'll be all right, Uncle," said Mother. "I'm sure Jack will find a job soon."

"Humph!" snorted Uncle Hendrick. "No, he will not. Not him. And not during these hard times."

Kit realized that her fists were clenched. Oooh! She wanted to run out onto the terrace and punch Uncle Hendrick. She hated it when he spoke about Dad that way. But Mother didn't say anything.

"And what will you do in the meantime?" Uncle Hendrick continued. "You should sell this house right away, though who'd buy it I can't imagine. Such foolish extravagance to buy it in the first place! You must owe the bank thousands of dollars."

"This is our home, Uncle," Kit heard Mother say. "We'll do whatever we can to keep it."

"Indeed!" said Uncle Hendrick. "And what might that be, if I may ask?"

Mother didn't answer.

"Just as I thought," said Uncle Hendrick smugly. "You haven't any idea. There's nothing you can do."

"Well," said Mother, "we could . . . take in boarders. Paying guests."

Kit felt as surprised as Uncle Hendrick sounded. "Boarders?" he gasped.

"Yes," said Mother. "It's perfectly respectable. We'll take in teachers, or nurses from the hospital."

Gosh! thought Kit. *Would you listen to Mother!*

But Uncle Hendrick had evidently heard enough. "Well, Margaret," he said. "All I can say is that if my sister, your dear mother, could see you now, it would break her heart." With that, Uncle Hendrick strode back to his car and drove away.

Kit ventured out onto the terrace. "Are we really going to take in boarders?" she asked Mother.

Mother smiled, and this time it was one of her real smiles that made Kit feel like smiling, too. "I surprised myself by saying that," said Mother. "I'm afraid I just wanted to shock Uncle Hendrick. But I rather like the idea." Mother laughed. "Yes," she said. "I like the idea a lot. It was a brainstorm."

"What's Dad going to say?" asked Kit.

"That," said Mother, "is a good question."

❀

Kit was not at all sure that she liked Mother's brainstorm. She wasn't crazy about the idea of strangers living in their house, especially considering the way Stirling had turned out. And what would the kids at school say when they found out Kit's family had to take in boarders?

Kit could tell that Dad didn't like the idea either.
Mother had first presented the idea to him in private,
of course, before she spoke about it again at dinner
that evening. Mrs. Howard was serving Stirling his
dinner up in their room, so only the family was at
the table.

"We have plenty of room," said Mother. "We should
put it to use."

"I don't think it's necessary," said Dad. "I'm making
every effort to find a job. Meanwhile—"

"Meanwhile this'll be a way for us to earn some
money," said Mother.

Dad sighed. "I hate the idea of you waiting on other
people, especially in our own home."

"We'll all chip in to help," answered Mother, in a
way that made it clear that the question of taking in
boarders was settled. Kit wasn't surprised. There was
never any way to stop Mother once she'd made up her
mind.

"But where will the boarders stay?" asked Kit.

"Charlie can move to the sleeping porch," said
Mother, "and we can put someone in his room."

"It's okay with me," said Charlie with a shrug.

"Thank you, dear," said Mother. "I'm also planning to find two schoolteachers or nurses to share the guest room."

Kit perked up. "Does that mean that Stirling and his mother will be leaving?" she asked. That'd be *one* good thing about Mother's plan at least!

"They'll stay," said Mother. "They'll be paying guests from now on."

"But *where* will they stay?" asked Kit.

Mother looked at Kit and said calmly, "Stirling and his mother will move into your room."

"*Mine?*" asked Kit, in a shocked, squeaky voice.

"Yes," said Mother. "We need them. They've got to stay if we want to make enough money to pay the mortgage every month. I figured it out."

"But Mother!" exclaimed Kit. "Where will *I* sleep?"

"I was thinking," said Mother briskly, "that you could move up to the attic. There's plenty of room up there."

The attic! thought Kit indignantly. She was being exiled to the hot, stuffy attic so that sniffle-nose Stirling could move into *her* room with his hankies and his meals on trays and his Vicks VapoRub!

Oh, oh, *oh!* In Kit's mind she saw her headline again, in letters that were four inches tall:

It's Not Fair!

❄

"But Kit," panted Ruthie, out of breath from climbing the stairs up to the attic, "you don't even like your room that much."

It was the next day. Kit and Ruthie were inspecting the attic. It smelled of mothballs, and it was gloomy because the windows were so dusty that the sun couldn't shine through them.

"You told me your room is too pink," Ruthie said. "Why are you so mad about moving out of it?"

"Because it was mine!" said Kit, knowing she sounded peevish. The fact that Ruthie was right, of course, just made Kit madder. "That room belonged to *me*, always, ever since I was a baby. And it just kills me to think that Stirling gets to have it. Why didn't *he* have to move up here?"

"I guess because his mother is paying rent now," said Ruthie calmly. She looked around. "It's not so bad up here," she said. "It's like the attic that Sara Crewe had to move into after she lost all her money. You know, in *The Little Princess*."

Kit felt very impatient with Ruthie and her princesses this morning! "Sara Crewe's room was transformed for her by that Indian guy," Kit said crossly. "Remember? He made it beautiful. He was practically magic about it."

"Your mother's practically magic about making things beautiful, too," said Ruthie. "She'll help you up here, right?"

"Right!" said Kit. But she was dead wrong.

That afternoon, while she was helping Mother make the beds, Kit asked her how they were going to fix up the attic.

Mother said, "I don't have time to help you right now, dear. I'm far too busy getting the rooms ready for the boarders." Mother's arms were full of sheets for the roll-away cot, which was being moved into Kit's old room for Stirling to sleep on. "After you help me, why don't you just poke around up there?" she said. "See what you can find."

Mother spoke in such a distracted manner that Kit's feelings were hurt. Mother had been *so* particular about every detail in Kit's pink room. But she didn't seem to give a hoot about Kit's attic.

Kit climbed slowly up the stairs to the attic. She stood in the middle of the room and looked around at the lumpy, dusty piles that surrounded her. In a far corner, she saw her old brown desk chair. She saw her old desk, too, hidden under a bumpy mattress and some boxes. Kit knelt next to one of the boxes and looked inside. *Now, if I were in a book,* Kit thought, *I'd find something wonderful in here.* But the box had only junk in it: a broken camera, a pair of binoculars and a compass that must have belonged to Dad in the war, a gooseneck lamp, and an old telephone, the kind that looked like a daffodil. *Old and useless,* thought Kit.

She took the compass out of the box and hung it around her neck. Then she sank down to the floor, overwhelmed by sadness. When she'd been wishing for change so that she could have a dramatic headline, she'd never imagined *this*! Terrible changes! And so many! And so fast! Dad had lost his job. She had lost her room. And in a way, they *were* going to lose their house. They'd still be living in it, but it wouldn't be the same when it was filled up with strangers. Nothing would *ever* be the same.

Kit almost never cried. She bit her lip now and fought back tears. Then, suddenly, Stirling's head appeared at the top of the stairs.

"What are you doing out of bed?" Kit asked, roughly brushing away a tear.

Kit could tell that Stirling knew she'd been crying, but all he said was, "I'm bringing this stuff from your room." He came all the way up the stairs and handed Kit a box. She noticed that the photo of Ernie Lombardi, wrinkled but smoothed flat, was on top.

"Thanks," said Kit.

"I brought you a tack, too," said Stirling. He gave Kit the tack and looked around. "I guess you can put Ernie Lombardi up anywhere you want to up here, can't you?" he said in his weirdly husky voice. Then he disappeared down the stairs.

After Stirling left, Kit looked down at the photograph. She felt oddly cheered to see it. *Old sniffle-nose Stirling is right*, she thought. *I guess I can put anything anywhere I want up here.*

Kit looked around the long, narrow attic. The ceiling

was steeply pitched. There were regular windows at each end of the room, and dormer windows that jutted out of the roof and made little pointy-roofed alcoves, each one about as wide as Kit was tall. The windows went almost all the way to the floor of the alcoves. Kit managed to open one of the heavy windows. She knelt down, stuck her head out, and came face-to-face with a leafy tree branch.

At that moment, Kit got a funny excited feeling. Suddenly, she knew exactly what she wanted to do.

❀

Over the next few days, Kit was glad that no one seemed to care what she was up to up in the attic. When she wasn't helping Mother downstairs, she hauled buckets of soapy water up there and scrubbed the windows till they sparkled. She swept the floor and pushed the boxes far to one end of the room. She had decided to use only half of the attic to live in and to pile junk in the other half. Finally the cleaning was done, and the fun part began.

In one alcove, Kit put her rolltop desk and her swivel chair. She put the gooseneck lamp on the desk, along with the telephone, the camera, and her typewriter. That was her newspaper office alcove.

In another alcove, Kit tacked up her photo of Ernie Lombardi. On a nail, she hung her catcher's mitt and the old binoculars. She figured she might need the binoculars if she ever went to a Reds game. That was her baseball alcove.

In the third alcove, Kit made bookshelves out of boards and arranged all her books on them. She found a huge chair that was losing its stuffing, and she shoved it into the alcove and softened it with a pillow. That was her reading alcove.

The last alcove was Kit's favorite. She put the lumpy mattress on an old bed frame and pushed the bed into the alcove with the pillow near the window. She surrounded the bed with some of Mother's potted plants. That was her tree house alcove.

❀

The very first night Kit slept in her tree house alcove, Mother came up to tuck her in. She sat on the edge of Kit's bed, and looked around the attic. Kit watched Mother's face carefully. She knew the attic was a far cry from Mother's idea of what a girl's room should look like.

"Well!" said Mother at last. "A place for every interest and every interest in its place. I can see that you've worked hard to make this attic your room. I'm proud of you, Kit."

"Thanks," said Kit.

"I'm sorry I haven't had time to help you," said Mother. "I'm afraid I've left you all on your own."

"That's okay," said Kit.

Mother kissed Kit's forehead. Then she picked up Kit's book. "Still reading *Robin Hood*?" she asked.

"Yup," said Kit. "*Robin Hood* gave me the idea to make a tree house alcove to sleep in." Kit also had plans for a swinging bridge to connect the window ledge to the tree just outside the window, but she didn't tell Mother. It was going to be a secret escape, like Robin Hood had.

"Good old Robin Hood," said Mother. "Robbing the rich to give to the poor."

Kit propped herself up on her elbows and looked at Mother. "Too bad there isn't any Robin Hood today," she said. "If rich people had to give some of their money to the poor, it would make the Depression better."

"It would help," said Mother. "But I don't think it would end the Depression."

"What will?" asked Kit.

"I don't know," said Mother. "Lots of things, I suppose. People will have to work hard. Use what they have. Face challenges. Stay hopeful." She looked around Kit's attic and smiled. "I guess they'll have to do sort of what you've done up here in your attic. They'll have to make changes and realize that changes can be good." Then she kissed Kit again. "Good night, dear," she said. "Don't read too late."

"I won't," said Kit. "Good night."

After Mother went downstairs, Kit flipped over onto her stomach and looked out the open window. She could hear the leaves rustling outside and see stars peeking through the branches. *'Changes Can Be Good,'* she thought. *That sounds like a headline to me.*

Messages

By the time Kit started back to school, three new boarders had moved into the Kittredges' house—a musician named Mr. Peck and two young nurses, Miss Hart and Miss Finney. The money they paid for their rooms and meals helped Kit's family. Kit knew that was a good change.

But with the new boarders plus Mrs. Howard and Stirling, the house felt much too crowded. And Kit's list of chores had gotten a whole lot longer, because all the extra people meant more cooking, cleaning, and laundry. Those were *not* good changes. It was almost a relief to head off to school every morning.

Almost. On this rainy November morning, the attic was cold, and Kit didn't want to get up. She shivered and burrowed deeper under her covers.

"Hey, Kit, wake up."

Kit opened one eye and saw her brother Charlie at
the foot of her bed. She put her pillow over her head
and groaned, "Go *away*."

"Can't do that," said Charlie cheerfully. "Not till
I'm sure you're up and at 'em." He turned on the lamp.
"Come on, Squirt. Time to get to work."

Kit groaned again, but she sat up. "I'm awake," she
yawned.

"Good," said Charlie. He tilted his head. "What's
that funny sound?"

Kit listened. *Plink. Plinkplinkplink!* "Oh," she said.
"The roof leaks."

"Why don't you ask Dad to fix it?" asked Charlie.
"I'm sure he could."

"Well, it only leaks when it rains," said Kit.

"No kidding," said Charlie.

"Besides, I like the plinking sound," Kit said. "It's
like someone's sending me a message in a secret code
that uses plinks instead of dots and dashes." In adventure stories, people often sent messages in secret codes,
and Kit was always on the lookout for excitement.

"*Plinkplinkplink*," said Charlie. "That means 'Get up,
Kit.'"

"Okay, okay!" laughed Kit as she got out of bed. "I get the message!"

"At last," said Charlie. "See you later." He waved and disappeared down the stairs. Charlie had to leave very early every day to get to his job loading newspapers onto trucks, but he always woke Kit and said good-bye before he left.

Kit dressed quickly. Mornings got off to a fast start at the Kittredge house these days. Mother was *very* particular about having breakfast ready on time for the boarders.

As Kit hurriedly tied her shoes, she saw that someone had moved her typewriter from one side of her desk to the other. *I bet Dad used my typewriter,* she thought. *He probably wrote a letter to ask about a job.* Kit sighed. She promised herself that the day Dad got a new job, she'd make a newspaper with a huge headline that said, 'Hurray for Dad! Bye-Bye, Boarders!' Kit could not *wait* for that day. She did not like having the boarders in the house *at all.*

The thought of that headline cheered Kit as she went downstairs to the second floor to face her morning chores. Her first stop was the bathroom, where she fished three of Dad's socks out of the laundry basket. Teetering first on one foot, then on the other, Kit put a sock over each shoe. She put the third sock over her right hand like a mitten. Then Kit propped the laundry basket against her hip and peeked out the door to be sure the coast was clear. It was. Kit took a running start, then *swoosh!* She skated down the hallway, dusting the floor with her sock-covered feet and giving the table in the hall a quick swipe with her sock-covered hand.

Kit skated fast. She could already hear the boarders rising and making the annoying noises they made every morning. As she skated past Mr. Peck's room, she heard him blowing his nose: *Honkhonk h-o-n-k! Honkhonk h-o-n-k!* It sounded to Kit like a goose honking the tune of "Jingle Bells." The two lady boarders were chirping to each other in twittery bursts of words and laughter. Next door to them, in what used to be Kit's room, Mrs. Howard was bleating and baaing over her son Stirling like a mother sheep over her lamb. *A chirp, chirp here and a baa, baa there! It's like living on Old MacDonald's Farm, for Pete's sake!* Kit thought crossly. She skated to the top of the stairs, sat, peeled off the socks, and put them back in the laundry basket. Then she climbed onto the banister and polished it by sliding down it sideways. She landed with a thud at the foot of the stairs and found a surprise waiting for her: Mother.

"Oh! Good morning, Mother!" said Kit.

Mother crossed her arms over her chest. "Is that how you do your chores every day?" she asked. "Skating and sliding?"

"Uh . . . well, yes," said Kit.

"No wonder the hallway is always so dusty. Not to mention Dad's socks," said Mother. She sighed a sigh that sounded weary for so early in the morning. "Dear, I thought you understood that we've all got to work hard to make our boarding house a success. Your chores are not a game. Is that clear?"

"Yes, Mother," said Kit.

"I'd appreciate it if you would dust more carefully from now on," said Mother. She managed a small smile. "And so would Dad's socks."

Kit felt sheepish. "Should I dust the hall again now?" she asked.

"I'm afraid there's no time," said Mother. "I'll try to get to it myself later. Right now I need your help with breakfast. The boarders will be down any minute. Come along."

"Okay," Kit said as she followed Mother into the kitchen. To herself she groused, *The boarders! It's all their fault. Mother never scolded me about things like dusting before they came, because I never had boring chores to do!* Kit knew her skate-and-slide method of dusting was slapdash, but she'd thought that nobody had noticed the dust left in the corners—except maybe persnickety Mrs. Howard. She should've known Mother would see it, too.

Mother wanted everything to be as nice as possible for the boarders. She insisted that the table be set beautifully for every meal. She went to great pains to make the food look nice, too, though there wasn't much of it. Dad went downtown nearly every day and brought home a loaf of bread and sometimes cans of fruits and vegetables. But even so, Mother had to invent ways to stretch the food so that there was enough. This morning Kit watched Mother cut the toasted bread into pretty triangles. Then, after Kit spooned oatmeal into a bowl, Mother put a thin slice of canned peach on top.

"That looks nice," said Kit. "The toast does, too."

"Just some tricks I've learned," Mother said. "Cutting the toast in triangles makes it look like there's more than there really is. And I'm hoping the peach slices will distract our guests from the fact that we've had oatmeal four times this week already. But it's cheap and it's filling."

"Humph!" said Kit as she plopped oatmeal into another bowl. "Oatmeal's good enough for *them*."

"Hush, Kit!" said Mother. She glanced at the door to the dining room as if the boarders might have heard. "You mustn't say that. We've got to keep our boarders happy. We need them to stay. In fact, we need more."

"*More* boarders?" asked Kit, horrified. "Oh, Mother, why?"

"Because," said Mother, sounding weary again, "even with Charlie's earnings and the rent from the boarders, we don't have enough money to cover our expenses. We need at least two more boarders to make ends meet."

"But where would we put them?" asked Kit. "No one would pay to share my attic. The roof leaks! And Charlie's sleeping porch is going to be freezing cold this winter."

"Yes," agreed Mother. "The sleeping porch should be enclosed, but we don't have any money for lumber."

"Anyway," said Kit, "it'd be silly to go changing the house all around and filling it with boarders when I bet Dad is going to get another job any day now. Didn't he say he's going downtown again today to have lunch with a business friend?"

"Mmmhmm," said Mother, taking the oatmeal spoon from Kit.

"Probably it's an interview!" said Kit. She crossed her fingers on both hands. "Oh, I hope Dad gets a job!" she wished aloud.

"That," said Mother, "would be a dream come true." She handed the heavy breakfast tray to Kit, took off her apron, and smoothed her hair. "Meanwhile, all we have going for us is this house and our own hard work. We must do everything we can to make sure our boarders stay. We can't let them see us worried and moping. So! Shoulders back, chin up, and put on a cheery morning face, please."

Kit forced her lips into a stiff smile.

"I guess that will have to do," said Mother briskly. She put on a smile too, pushed open the door, and

walked into the dining room like an actress making
an entrance on a stage. Dad and all the boarders were
seated at the table. "Good morning, everyone!" Mother
said.

"Good morning!" they all answered.

Kit's smile turned into a real one when she saw Dad,
who was wearing his best suit and looking very hand-
some. He winked at her as if to send her a message that
said, *It really is a good morning now that I've seen you.*

Miss Hart and Miss Finney cooed with pleasure
when Kit set their peachy oatmeal before them. Kit was
careful not to spill. Their starched nurses' uniforms
were as white as blank pieces of paper before a story
was written on them. *I bet Miss Hart and Miss Finney
have plenty of interesting stories to tell about their patients at
the hospital,* thought Kit. *Maybe they've had daring nursing adventures, like Florence Nightingale and Clara Barton.
What great newspaper headlines those adventures would
make!*

Then Kit scolded herself for being curious. Miss
Hart and Miss Finney must remain blank pages! Kit
did not want to like them. She did not want to be interested in them or in Mr. Peck, either, even though he

played a double bass as big as a bear and had a beard and was so tall he reminded Kit of Little John in her favorite book, *Robin Hood*. They would probably all turn out to be dull anyway, just as disappointing as tidy Mrs. Howard and skinny Stirling. They were *not* friends. They were only boarders, and they wouldn't be around for very long. As soon as Dad got a new job, they'd leave. Kit thought back to the wish she'd made and rewrote it in her head. *I should have added the word* ***soon****, she thought. I hope Dad gets a job* ***soon***.

As Kit sat down at her place, she saw Dad slip his toast onto Stirling's plate. Stirling's mother saw, too, and started to fuss. "Oh, Mr. Kittredge!" said Mrs. Howard to Dad. "You're too generous! And Stirling's digestion is so delicate! He can't eat so much breakfast. It's a shame to waste it."

"Don't worry, Mrs. Howard," joked Dad. "Stirling's just helping me be a member of the Clean Plate Club. I'm having lunch with a friend today. I don't want to ruin my appetite."

Stirling didn't say a word. But Kit noticed that he wolfed down his own toast and Dad's, too, pretty fast. *Delicate digestion, my eye*, thought Kit.

"Goodness, Mr. Kittredge," Miss Finney piped up. "Last night at dinner you said you weren't hungry because you'd had a big lunch. Those lunches must be feasts!"

"They are indeed," said Dad.

Just then, Mother brought in the morning mail. She handed a couple of letters to Dad and one fat envelope to Miss Hart, who got a letter from her boyfriend in Boston practically every day. Kit was trying to imagine what Miss Hart's boyfriend had to say to her in those long letters when Mother said, "Why, Stirling, dear, look! This letter is for you."

Everyone was quiet as Mother handed Stirling the letter. Even his mother was speechless for once. The tips of Stirling's ears turned as pink as boiled shrimp. He looked at the envelope with his name and address typed on it, then eagerly ripped the envelope open, tearing it apart in his haste to get the letter out and read it.

Mrs. Howard recovered. "Who's it from, lamby?" she asked.

Stirling smiled a watery, timid-looking smile. "It's from Father," he answered. His odd husky voice sounded unsure, as if he himself could hardly believe what he was saying.

"My land!" exclaimed Mrs. Howard, pressing one hand against her heart. "A letter at last! What does he say?"

Stirling read the typewritten letter aloud. "'Dear Son, I haven't got a permanent address yet. I'll write to you when I do, and I'll send more money as soon as I can. Give my love to Mother. Love, Father.'" Stirling handed two ten-dollar bills to his mother. "He sent us this."

"Wow!" exclaimed Kit. "Twenty dollars? That's a lot of money!"

Miss Finney and Miss Hart murmured their agreement, and Mr. Peck put down his coffee cup in amazement.

Mrs. Howard was overcome with happiness. In a weak voice she said to Mother, "Margaret, take this." She tried to give Mother one of the ten-dollar bills. "You've been so kind to us. You must share in our lucky day."

"Oh, but—" Mother began.

"I insist," said Mrs. Howard.

Mother hesitated. Then she said, "Thank you." She put the ten-dollar bill in her pocket.

After that, everyone started talking at once about Stirling's startling letter. Everyone but Stirling, that is. Kit saw Stirling read his father's message once more, and then fold the letter very small and hold it in his closed hand.

❦

After breakfast, Dad sat at the kitchen table reading the want ads in the newspaper while Kit and Mother washed the dishes. "Mr. Howard must be doing all right if he can send his wife twenty dollars," Dad said from behind the newspaper. "Maybe Chicago is the place to go. Maybe there are jobs there."

"Chicago *is* a bigger city than Cincinnati," said Mother.

"We'd move to Chicago?" asked Kit. She didn't like the idea of leaving her home and her friends.

"No," said Dad, putting the paper down. "Only I would go."

Kit spun around from the sink so quickly that her wet hand left a trail of soapsuds on the kitchen floor.

"You'd go without us?" she asked, shocked. "You'd leave us? Oh, Dad, you can't!"

"Now Kit, calm down," said Dad. "It's just an idea. I haven't said I'll go. But if nothing turns up here by Thanksgiving . . ."

"Thanksgiving?" interrupted Kit. "That's only two weeks away!"

"You know how hard your father's been looking for a job here in Cincinnati," said Mother. "Ever since August."

"And he'll find one," said Kit. She looked at her father. "Won't you, Dad? One of those business friends you have lunch with is sure to offer you a job any day now, right?"

"Kit, sweetheart," Dad started to answer, then stopped. He picked up the paper and went back to his reading. "Right," he said. "Any day now."

As Kit turned back to the dishes, she thought, *When I wished for Dad to get a job soon, I didn't mean in Chicago!* In her head, she rewrote the message of her wish again. Now it was: *I hope Dad gets a job **soon**, and **here in Cincinnati.***

Pilgrims and Indians

✸ CHAPTER 6 ✸

As they walked to school that morning, Kit told Ruthie about changing her wish for Dad. The girls huddled under Ruthie's umbrella. They ignored Stirling, who trailed along behind them like a puny, pitiful puppy. "I didn't realize a wish had to be so specific," said Kit.

"Oh, yes," said Ruthie. "You have to be *very* careful what you say in a wish. Otherwise it'll come true, but not the way you meant it to. That happens a lot in fairy tales." Ruthie had read hundreds of fairy tales because she was interested in princesses. "Also, you usually have to work hard to *deserve* a wish to come true. You have to do something brave or impossible, or make a giant, noble sacrifice. And you have to wait. Wishes take time. Years, in some cases."

"Thanksgiving's only two weeks from now," said

Kit. "I'm afraid that if Dad doesn't get a job here by then, he'll go away to Chicago."

"Chicago," repeated Ruthie. "He might as well go to the moon."

"I don't want *Dad* to leave," said Kit. "I want the *boarders* to leave."

Ruthie tugged on one of the straps of Kit's book bag and tilted her head toward Stirling. Kit realized that once again she'd spoken without thinking. She was pretty sure that Stirling already knew she wanted him and the other boarders to leave. Still, it wasn't nice to say so in front of him. Kit wouldn't have if she'd re-membered that he was there. He was just so *invisible*.

All morning at school Kit tried not to think about how awful it would be to watch the boarders sitting around the table gobbling Thanksgiving turkey if she knew that Dad was going to leave. She could hardly bear listening to Roger, a show-offy boy in her class, answer a question about the first Thanksgiving that their teacher, Mr. Fisher, had asked.

"The first Thanksgiving was in 1621," said Roger. "The Pilgrims invited the Indians to a feast to celebrate their successful harvest. We have turkey at Thanksgiving because the Pilgrims served the Indians four wild turkeys, and we call it Thanksgiving because the Indians were thankful to the Pilgrims for being generous and sharing their food."

Kit couldn't stand it. She shot her hand up into the air and waved it.

"Yes, Kit?" said Mr. Fisher.

"Roger's got the story backwards," said Kit. "It's called Thanksgiving because the Pilgrims gave the feast to thank the Indians."

Roger snorted.

Kit wasn't the least bit intimidated by Roger. "The Pilgrims would've starved to death if it weren't for the Indians," she said. "The Indians taught the Pilgrims to plant corn and gave them supplies and help. I think that was pretty nice of the Indians, considering that the Pilgrims had barged into their land where they'd been living happily by themselves for a long time." As Kit spoke, she realized that this year, more than ever before, she had tremendous sympathy for the Indians. She knew how it felt to have a bunch of strangers living with you and eating your food and expecting your help when you didn't want them there in the first place!

"Well!" said Mr. Fisher. "Thank you, Kit."

It made Kit feel a little better to have pleased Mr. Fisher. She liked him, but they had gotten off on the wrong foot the first day of school when Mr. Fisher called on Kit to read aloud in reading group. Kit hadn't known what page they were on because she'd read ahead and was busy thinking up better endings to the stories.

Mr. Fisher was cross with her then, but he was happy with her now. "Kit makes a good point," he said. "The Indians took pity on the Pilgrims and shared what little they had. It's important to help both friends and strangers when times are hard. We see this all around us today, because of the Depression. Who can give me examples of ways that our families and friends and neighbors are helping one another, and strangers, too?"

"When hoboes come to our back door," said Ruthie, "my mother always gives them sandwiches and coffee."

"At our church there's a box of old shoes for people to take if they need them," said a boy named Tom.

"My cousin sent me a winter coat she'd outgrown," said a girl named Mabel.

Kit was surprised to see Stirling raise his hand. He'd almost never done so before. Stirling was new to the class and the school because he had moved into Kit's house only last summer. He didn't know anyone but Kit and Ruthie, and he was so quiet he was easy to forget.

"Sometimes people get kicked out of their house because they can't pay the rent," Stirling said in his deep voice that always surprised Kit, coming as it did from such a pip-squeak. "And friends are nice and invite them to live in their house with them."

"Oh, so that's why you live with Kit," brayed Roger. "I thought you two were married!"

The class snickered as Roger made kissing noises. Stirling slouched in his seat. Kit shook her fist at Roger, but she was mad at Stirling, too. *Stirling should have kept his mouth shut!* she thought.

"That will do, Roger," said Mr. Fisher. "I'll wait for quiet, boys and girls." He waited until the snickering stopped, then asked, "Who can give me more examples of how we're helping one another?"

"Soup kitchens serve free meals to people who can't buy food," said a girl named Dorothy. "And some soup kitchens also give people groceries to take home to their families."

"Yes," said Mr. Fisher. "Now, as you all know, Thanksgiving is coming soon. I'd like our class to do its part to help the hungry. So if you can, please bring in an item of food. It doesn't have to be anything big. An apple or a potato will do. I know most of us don't have much food to spare. But if we all chip in, we can make a Thanksgiving basket and donate it to a soup kitchen."

The students murmured among themselves, but without much enthusiasm. They'd all seen soup kitchens with long lines of people waiting outside them. Kit had once seen a man in a soup line faint on the street from hunger. She knew that soup kitchens were for people who had been without work for so long that they had no money or hope or pride left, and who were so desperate that they had to accept free food.

"My father says that people who go to soup kitchens should be ashamed," said Roger, full of bluster. "They're bums."

"They're not bums," said Ruthie. "Most of them are perfectly nice, normal people who happen to be down on their luck. I think we should feel sorry for them."

"My father says they're just too lazy to work," said Roger. "And now that Franklin Roosevelt's been elected, people will expect the government to take care of them. My father says it'll ruin our country."

Kit grew hot under the collar listening to Roger and thinking of how hard Dad was trying to find a job. "People aren't too lazy to work," she said. "They'd work if they could find a job. But jobs are hard to find."

Mr. Fisher nodded. "Right here in Cincinnati," he said, "one out of three workers is unemployed, which means they don't have a job. One out of three. What fraction is that?"

"One-third," said Tom.

"That's correct," said Mr. Fisher.

One out of three? thought Kit. Unemployment was a lot worse than she'd thought! Just for a shivery second, her absolute confidence that Dad would find a job in Cincinnati was shaken a little bit. Maybe he really would have to go to Chicago! Then Kit spoke to herself firmly. *No!* she thought. *Dad is different. He **will** find a job. Any day now. He said so.*

"These are hard times," said Mr. Fisher. "That's why it's especially important to remember the example of the Indians and the Pilgrims. We all have friends or relatives who're struggling to make ends meet. This year many of us will have to do without some of the things we've had in years past."

"But Mr. Fisher," Mabel asked, "we're still going to have a Thanksgiving pageant this year, aren't we?"

"Yes, of course," said Mr. Fisher.

Now the class buzzed with excitement. Everyone loved the pageant!

Mr. Fisher crossed his arms. "I need your attention, boys and girls," he said. The children shushed one another, and Mr. Fisher continued. "The sixth-graders will be the Pilgrims," he said. "The fifth-graders will be the Indians. Our fourth grade is responsible for the scenery." Mr. Fisher held up a drawing. "Here's a drawing of the backdrop we'll paint."

The drawing showed four giant turkeys and a huge cornucopia with fruits and vegetables spilling out. The turkeys' feathers were all different colors, and they were not just painted on. They were made out of bits of paper cut to look like real feathers, and they were glued onto the turkeys.

"That's good!" said Tom.

"Yes, it is, isn't it?" said Mr. Fisher.

"Who drew it?" asked Dorothy.

"Stirling," said Mr. Fisher.

Everyone twisted around to stare at Stirling. For the second time that day, Stirling slouched down in his seat. But this time, no one was snickering. Everyone, including Kit, was gaping at Stirling in astonishment.

❀

At lunch Ruthie said, "Stirling is really good at drawing, isn't he, Kit?"

Kit shrugged. "I guess so," she said. She was still annoyed with Stirling for speaking in class and embarrassing her in front of everybody.

"Shh!" said Dorothy. "Here he comes now!"

Stirling was walking toward Kit, his knickers ballooning out over his spindly legs. Kit and Stirling had to share a lunch tin, and every day Stirling came over to the girls' side of the lunchroom to get his sandwich from Kit. Usually, the girls at the table completely ignored Stirling. But today when he came over, several girls squeaked, "Hi, Stirling."

Stirling blushed pinker than ever. "Hi," he mumbled. He took his sandwich and scuttled back to the boys' side. Unfortunately, Roger had spotted Stirling with Kit. He began to whistle "Here Comes the Bride." Kit glowered at Roger, who batted his eyelashes at her across the lunchroom.

"Hey, Kit," said Ruthie, trying to distract her. "Good news! There's some wood left over from our new garage. My father said that you and I can use it for our tree house."

"That's great!" said Kit. She had been sketching tree houses and hoping to build one ever since she'd read *Robin Hood*. She loved the tree houses that Robin and his men built high in the branches of the trees in Sherwood Forest. Kit knew her family had absolutely no money to spend on something as unnecessary as wood for a tree house. So it was lucky that Ruthie's father, who still had a job, was giving away the leftover wood.

"I was thinking," said Ruthie, "you know how your tree house sketches haven't ever really turned out very well?"

"Yes," Kit admitted honestly.

"Well, why don't we ask Stirling to draw a plan for us?" asked Ruthie.

"No!" Kit said. "Gosh, Ruthie! If we let him plan a tree house for us, then when it's built he'll want to come in it and we'll have to let him. He's already invaded my real house. I don't want him in our tree house, too!"

"Okay, okay," said Ruthie. "Don't get all worked up. The tree house doesn't even *exist* yet!"

"I'll ask Dad to help us," said Kit. "He loves building things."

"Sure!" said Ruthie. She grinned. "And he'll be so busy building our tree house, he'll forget all about going away!"

Kit grinned back. "Right!" she said. "How soon can we get that wood?"

Spilling the Beans

圏 CHAPTER 7 圏

 few days later, Kit's class was on the stage
in the school auditorium working on the
backdrop for the Thanksgiving pageant.
Stirling had drawn the outline on big sheets of paper
that were pinned to the curtains at the back of the
stage. The boys in the class were painting in the fruits
and vegetables and the cornucopia. The girls were cutting out paper turkey feathers. Stirling was standing on
a stool, gluing the finished feathers onto the outlines of
the giant turkeys.

Mr. Fisher was far away, up in the balcony
wrestling with the spotlights, and Roger was taking
advantage of his absence by being a general pain. He
came over and jabbed Stirling with his paintbrush.
"So, Stirling," he said, "when's the wedding for you
and Kit?"

It was as if Stirling hadn't heard Roger. He stepped down off his stool and calmly began brushing glue onto another batch of turkey feathers.

Roger turned his back on Stirling. "Hey, Kit," he said. "What's the matter with your boyfriend? He's awful quiet."

"Stirling is *not* my boyfriend," snapped Kit. "He and his mother *pay* to live at our house. They're *boarders.*"

"Oh yeah!" Roger drawled. "That's right." He plopped himself down on the stool that Stirling had been using. Loudly and slowly, so that everyone could hear him, Roger said, "I heard that your family is so hard up you're running a boarding house now." He smirked. "And *you're* the maid."

"I am not!" Kit denied hotly. Of course, she *had* been feeling like a maid lately. But she'd never give Roger satisfaction by admitting it.

"That's not what I heard," Roger taunted. "Here's you." He pretended that his paintbrush was a maid's feather duster and he used it to brush some imaginary dust off his arms. Then he stood up, turned, and started to swagger away.

It was then that Kit saw the giant turkey feathers

stuck to the seat of Roger's pants! Kit touched Ruthie's arm and pointed at Roger.

Ruthie chortled when she saw the feathers. "Hey, look, everybody!" she called out happily, pointing to Roger's bottom. "Look at Roger—Mr. Turkeypants!"

Everyone looked. The girls screamed with laughter and the boys whistled and clapped. "Hey, Turkey-pants!" Ruthie hooted. "Gobble, gobble!" Kit realized with surprise that Stirling must have sneaked the gluey feathers onto the stool just as Roger sat down so they'd stick to his pants when he stood up.

Roger also realized that Stirling was the one who'd tricked him. "You think you're pretty smart, don't you, Stirling?" he said furiously as he pulled off the gluey feathers. "Sticking your stupid turkey feathers on me. Well, at least *my* father hasn't flown the coop and disappeared like yours has!"

By now the whole class was gathered around Kit, Ruthie, Stirling, and Roger. They all looked at Stirling, waiting to hear what he'd say to Roger.

But Stirling didn't say anything, and his silence exasperated Kit. "For your information, birdbrain," she said to Roger, "Stirling's father sent him a letter from

Chicago just a few days ago." She paused for impact. "And it had twenty dollars in it! His mother gave ten dollars to my mother."

Everyone gasped. *"Twenty dollars!"* they whispered in amazement.

"Well," sneered Roger. "That's good news for *your* family then, Kit, since your father doesn't have a job *or* any money. My father says your dad used up all of his savings to pay the people who worked at his car dealership, which was stupid. No wonder no one will offer him a job."

"That's not true!" said Kit, outraged. "My father has job interviews all the time. Almost every day he has big, fancy lunches and meetings about jobs. He'll get one any day now. He said so."

"No, he won't," said Roger. "Nobody wants your father."

With that, Roger shoved his armful of sticky turkey feathers at Kit, who shoved them right back. Kit was so angry and shoved so hard that Roger staggered backward, lost his balance, and fell against a ladder that had a bucket of white paint on it. Everyone shrieked in horror and delight as the can fell over, splattering

white paint on the backdrop and clonking Roger on
the head! White paint spilled over Roger's hair and face
and shoulders and back and arms. It ran in rivers down
Roger, striping his legs and his socks and pooling into
white puddles around his shoes.

"Arrgghh!" Roger roared. He swiped his hand
across his face to clear the paint out of his eyes and
lunged for Kit.

But at that very instant, Mr. Fisher appeared.
"Stop!" he shouted.

Roger stopped. Everyone was quiet.

Mr. Fisher frowned as he surveyed the white mess.
"Who's responsible for this?" he demanded.

"Not me!" said Roger. "Stirling started it. He stuck
feathers on me. And then Ruthie called me Mr. Tur—a
stupid name—and Kit shoved me into the ladder. *They*
did it, not me. They—"

Mr. Fisher held up his hand. "Quiet," he said.
"Roger, go to the boys' room and clean yourself up.
Boys and girls, I want you to go back to the classroom
and sit silently at your desks. Kit, Ruthie, and Stirling,
you three stay here. I want to talk to you."

Roger scuttled past Kit on his way out. "*Now* you're

going to get it," he hissed at her, sounding pleased. "*Now* you'll be sorry!"

Kit lifted her chin. "I'm not sorry I shoved you, Roger," she said. "I'd do it again, no matter what the punishment is. I'd shove anyone who says anything mean about my dad!"

"So watch out!" added Ruthie for good measure.

Roger made a face. But for once, he made no smart remark in reply.

❉

When Kit, Ruthie, and Stirling were walking home from school later, the girls agreed that Mr. Fisher's punishment was not too terrible, really. They'd had to clean up the stage, and they were going to have to spend their recess time for the rest of the week helping Stirling redo the backdrop where white paint had spattered on it. Mr. Fisher had also decided that Kit, Ruthie, and Stirling would deliver the class's Thanksgiving basket to a soup kitchen while the rest of the class was watching the Thanksgiving pageant.

"The only bad part of the punishment is missing the pageant," said Ruthie. "Especially because we have to go to a soup kitchen instead."

"The worst part to me is that loudmouth Roger isn't being punished," said Kit. "It's not fair. He's the one who started the whole fight."

"Don't worry," said Ruthie. "In fairy tales, bad guys like Roger always get their comeuppance in the end. Everyone finds out the truth eventually."

That reminded Kit of something. "Uh, Stirling," she said. "It would probably be better if we didn't say any-thing about this . . . this situation when we get home. My mother might get a little upset if she found out."

"Mine, too," said Stirling. His voice was serious, but Kit saw a little ghost of a smile flicker across his face. She understood. They both knew that Stirling's mother would go into absolute *fits* if she found out her little lamb had been part of a fight. And she'd surely come swooping down to school and insist that he couldn't possibly go to a soup kitchen. Think of the germs!

"You know, Stirling," said Ruthie. "I think you're being pretty nice about this whole thing. After all, it was your drawing that was ruined by all that paint."

Another smile flickered across Stirling's face. "Too bad the first Thanksgiving didn't take place during a blizzard," he said in his low voice. "Then Roger could have been the Abominable Snowman in the pageant."

Ruthie laughed. And Kit did, too.

❈

Stirling knew how to keep quiet. He did not spill the beans about the spilled paint, the fight, or the punishment. So when the day came for the trip to the soup kitchen, Kit and Stirling went off to school as if it were a normal morning. They did bring Kit's wagon with them, but the grownups were too busy to notice.

After an early lunch at school, the rest of the class went to the pageant. Mr. Fisher helped Kit, Ruthie, and Stirling put the Thanksgiving basket into the wagon. It was heavy. Students had brought potatoes, beans, and apples. There were a few jars of preserves and six loaves of bread. Kit and Stirling brought a can of fruit, and Ruthie, whose family still had plenty of money, brought in a turkey that weighed twenty pounds.

"The soup kitchen is down on River Street," said Mr. Fisher. "After you deliver the basket, you may go home." He paused. "Happy Thanksgiving," he said.

Then he hurried off so he wouldn't miss the beginning of the pageant.

Kit, Ruthie, and Stirling set out. It was a cold day. The sky was the grayish brown color of a dirty potato, and soon it began to spit rain. Ruthie propped her umbrella up in the wagon to keep the basket dry. Kit's shoes were wet through, and her wrists were wet and chapped because her arms were too long for her coat sleeves. Her shoulders ached from pulling the heavy wagon. But Kit was not the kind of girl who wasted time feeling sorry for herself. Instead, she made up her mind to pretend that she was a newspaper reporter. As she walked along, she imagined how she would write about the people and things she was seeing.

"I'll take a turn pulling the wagon now," Ruthie offered after a while.

"Thanks," said Kit. She smiled at Ruthie, who looked like a damp, overstuffed couch in her new winter coat. "This whole thing is kind of an adventure, isn't it?"

"Sure," said Ruthie, after only the tiniest hesitation. "We're like the bedraggled princess in 'The Princess and the Pea.'"

Kit grinned. *Good old Ruthie,* she thought. *She has a princess for every occasion.*

"No one who sees us would know that this is a punishment," Kit said. "It doesn't look like one, or feel like one, either."

"No," said Ruthie. "Especially since Roger's not with us."

The girls giggled.

But they stopped giggling when they turned the corner onto River Street and saw the line outside the soup kitchen. It was four people across, and it stretched from the door of the soup kitchen all the way to the end of the block. The people stood shoulder to shoulder, hunched against the rain. The brims of their hats were pulled low over their faces as if they were ashamed to be there and did not want to be recognized. The buildings that lined the street were as gray as the rain. They seemed to slump together as if they were ashamed, too.

"Oh my," said Ruthie quietly.

Stirling didn't say anything, but he moved up to be next to the girls.

Kit prided herself on being brave, but even she was daunted by the dreary scene before her. She squared her shoulders. "Let's go around to the back door," she suggested. "That's probably the right place to make a delivery."

Kit led the way down a small alley and around to the rear of the building. She knocked on the back door. No one answered. Kit lifted the basket out of the wagon. She took a deep breath, pushed the door open, and stepped inside. Stirling and Ruthie followed her. When they went in, they saw why no one had answered Kit's knock. It was very busy.

People were rushing about with huge, steamy kettles of soup, trays of sandwiches, and pots of hot coffee. A swinging door separated the kitchen from the room where the food was served and the groceries were given away.

One lady saw Kit and the others and stopped short. She peered through the steam rising off the soup she carried and asked, "May I help you?"

"We're from Mr. Fisher's class," said Kit. "We have a Thanksgiving basket to donate."

"Oh, yes!" said the lady. "You're expected. Bless you! As you can see, my hands are full. You'll have to unpack the basket yourselves. Leave the turkey and the potatoes and all here in the kitchen. We'll use them to make tomorrow's soup. But bring the canned goods and the loaves of bread out front now. You can give them away."

Kit, Ruthie, and Stirling did as they were told. After they unloaded the basket, they pushed through the swinging door from the kitchen to the front room, which was crowded with people. It smelled of soup and coffee. At round tables in the center of the room, people sat eating and drinking. Some talked quietly. But most of the people kept a polite silence, as if they did not want to call attention to themselves or make themselves known to anyone around them. Along one side of the room, there was a long table with people lined up in front of it. Kit could see only their backs as they stood patiently, holding bowls and spoons, waiting for soup to be served to them. Across the room there was another long table where a lady was handing out groceries and loaves of bread for people to take home. Rather shyly, Kit, Ruthie, and Stirling went over, put their food on the table, and stood next to her.

"Thanks," said the lady. "Please give the bread to the people as they pass by."

Kit, Ruthie, and Stirling kept their eyes on the bread as they handed it out. It was kinder and more respectful not to look into the faces of the people, who seemed grateful but embarrassed to be accepting free food. Most of them kept their eyes down, too. Kit felt very, very sorry for them as they took their bread, murmured their thanks, and moved away. *All of these people have sad stories to tell,* she thought. *They weren't always hungry and hopeless like they are now. How humiliating this must be for them!*

The lady handing out the groceries seemed to know some of the people. "Well, hello!" she said to one man. "You're here a little later than usual today."

Kit handed the man his bread.

"Thank you," he said.

Kit looked up, bewildered.

It was Dad.

Kit's Hard Times

it!" Dad gasped.

Kit couldn't breathe. She felt as if she had been punched hard in the stomach. Shock, disbelief, and a sickening feeling of terrible shame shot through her as she stared at Dad.

Suddenly, Kit could bear no more. She pushed past Ruthie and Stirling and bolted through the swinging doors. She ran through the kitchen and past the stoves with kettles of soup that had billowing clouds of steam rising from them. She burst out the back door into the alley. Once she was outside, her legs felt wobbly, and she sagged against the hard brick wall.

In a moment, Ruthie and Stirling were beside her. "Kit?" said Ruthie gently. "Are you okay?"

Kit nodded. She looked at Ruthie. "Is my dad still . . ." she began.

"Your dad left," said Ruthie. "He said he'd talk to you at home."

Kit took a shaky breath.

"Come on," said Ruthie. "Let's go." Stirling grabbed the wagon handle, and they started down the alley with the empty wagon rattling and banging noisily behind them. Slowly, miserably, and without talking, the three of them walked together until they came to the end of Ruthie's driveway. They stopped next to the stack of lumber left over from the new garage, and Ruthie turned her sad face toward Kit. "Listen," she said. "Everything's going to be all right."

"All right?" Kit repeated. She shivered. "No, Ruthie," she said. "Everything's *not* going to be all right. My father hasn't been having job interviews. He's been going to a soup kitchen. He had to, just to get something to *eat*, to get food for our *family* to eat." Kit's voice shook. "Dad's not going to get a job here in Cincinnati. Maybe he would have a better chance of finding one in Chicago. I guess . . ." Kit faltered, then went on. "I guess now I hope that he *will* go."

"No, you don't," said Stirling in his husky voice.

Kit frowned. "What do *you* know about what I

want?" she asked. "*Your* father is in Chicago, sending you letters with money stuck in them!"

"No," said Stirling. His gray eyes looked straight at Kit. "He isn't."

"What are you talking about?" asked Kit. "I saw the money!"

"That was *my* twenty dollars," Stirling said. "My father gave it to me before he left. He told me to save it for an emergency." Stirling sighed, and then he poured out the whole story. "My mother hasn't been able to pay any rent since we moved in," he said. "I offered her the twenty dollars lots of times, but she always said no. Then, a few weeks ago, she told me that we were going to have to leave your house. I knew it was because she was ashamed to stay any longer without paying. She wouldn't feel so bad if she could help with the housework, but your mother won't let her. I figured if I could trick her into taking the twenty dollars, she might use it for rent. So I made her think it came in a letter from my father."

Kit squinted at Stirling, trying to understand. "You sneaked the money into the letter?" she asked.

Stirling shook his head. "No," he said. "It's worse

than that." He paused. "I wrote the letter myself. I typed it on your typewriter."

"*What?*" Kit and Ruthie asked together.

"The truth . . ." Stirling hesitated. "The truth is, I don't know where my father is," he said. "But I'm pretty sure he's never coming back here to my mother and me. He flew the coop, as Roger said."

"Oh, no," Ruthie sighed.

Kit felt her hands clench into fists.

"So that's how I know that you don't want your dad to go away, Kit," said Stirling earnestly. "No matter what, it's better to have your dad at home. No matter how bad or hopeless things are, you don't want him to leave."

Kit sat down hard in the wagon. She held her head in her hands.

"Stirling," said Ruthie, "you'd better tell your mom what you did."

Stirling nodded. It was as if he'd used up all his words.

Ruthie walked up her driveway backward, waving good-bye until she went inside her house. Kit stood up tiredly. As she trudged slowly home with the wagon and Stirling behind her, a new thought presented itself. *When Stirling tells his mother about the letter and the money, they'll leave,* she thought. She walked up the steps and opened her front door. *They won't live here in our house anymore.*

Of course, Kit had wanted Stirling and his fussbudgety mother to leave ever since they'd arrived. But now . . . It was very peculiar. Now that it was about to happen, Kit did not feel glad. She stood in the front hall, which smelled of wet wool coats and dripped with umbrellas, and watched Stirling head upstairs to the room he and his mother shared.

"Is that you, lamby?" Mrs. Howard called. "Did you wipe your feet?"

Stirling looked back over his shoulder at Kit, and a quicksilvery smile slipped across his face. Then he turned away and climbed the rest of the stairs.

Slowly, Kit took off her coat and headed upstairs to change out of her school clothes. As she passed by Mother and Dad's room, the door opened.

"Kit," said Dad. "Come in here, please. I'd like to talk to you."

Kit went in and sat on the desk chair.

"I've already told your mother about what happened today," said Dad. "I owed her an apology, and I owe you and Charlie one, too. I'm sorry I misled all of you. I should have told you what I was really doing." Dad walked over to the window and looked out. "I've been going to the soup kitchen for weeks now, to eat and to get food to bring home. We've been so short of food. It was the only way I could contribute to the household."

"Are we . . . are we really that poor?" asked Kit, almost in a whisper.

"Yes," said Dad. "We are. But I didn't want any of you to know. That's why I pretended not to be hungry here at home. I'd have lunch at the soup kitchen, and then I could give my breakfast or dinner away to make our groceries stretch further." Dad turned to face Kit. "I shouldn't have led you to believe that I'd find a job here in Cincinnati soon. I guess my only excuse is that I wanted it to be true."

Kit went to stand next to Dad. He put his arm around her shoulder.

"But," said Dad, "it's time for me—for all of us—to face the truth. And the truth is that there's nothing for

me to do here. There's no point in studying the want
ads in the newspapers every day for a job that's never
going to appear. So your mother and I have decided.
I'm going to Chicago."

"Oh, Dad!" cried Kit. "You're not going to Chicago
because of that letter from Stirling's father, are you?
Because—"

Dad held up his hand to stop her. "I'm going," he
said, "because there's really no alternative. We don't
have room in the house to take in as many boarders as
we need. If I go to Chicago, maybe I can find a job and
send a little money home."

"I don't want you to go, Dad," Kit said desperately.

"You'll have to write to me and tell me what happens after I leave," Dad said, smiling a small smile.
"It'll be like the old days. Remember the newspapers
you used to make for me? I loved them so much. When
I'm gone, will you write newspapers and send them to
me so I won't feel so far away?"

Kit nodded slowly.

"That's my girl," said Dad. "You were my reporter
during the good times. I need you to be my reporter
during the hard times, too."

Hard times, thought Kit dully as she left Dad and walked down the hallway. The odor of onions frying rose up from the kitchen, and Kit knew that Mother must be making another one of the odd sauces she made so often nowadays—one that was meant to stretch a small piece of meat to feed a crowd. Kit heard Miss Hart and Miss Finney laughing in their room and Mr. Peck teaching Charlie to play his big double bass fiddle. She thought about the chores waiting for her that absolutely had to be done. Mother needed her to set the table for dinner and scrub the potatoes and put them in the oven to bake. Then there was laundry to iron and fold and put away, all before dinner. *This is it,* Kit thought. *This is the truth of my life now. Maybe forever.*

With heavy, defeated steps, Kit climbed the stairs to the attic. How foolish she had been to think that her life was going to go back to the way it used to be! Kit sank into her desk chair. She cleared a space between her typewriter and a pile of papers and rested her head on her arms. She had been wrong about so many things! Instead of resenting the boarders, she should have been grateful for them. Instead of wanting them

to leave, she should have been trying to figure out a
way to fit more boarders into the house. Because . . .
Kit felt pinpricks of fear up her spine. Because there
was no guarantee that Dad would be able to find a job
in Chicago, either. What would become of her family?
How would they have enough money for food and
clothes and heat? Would they be so poor they'd be
kicked out of their house?

Oh, I wish we had room for more boarders! Kit thought
passionately. *Then Dad could stay. If Ruthie's right about
wishes, and you have to work hard to deserve them, then I
promise to work as hard as I possibly can to make this one
come true.*

Kit felt a drop of water on her hand. She looked
up and saw a new leak in the roof, right above her
desk. Drops of water plopped onto the papers next to
her. Kit saw that the drops had blurred one of her tree
house sketches. *Oh well, what difference does it make?* she
thought, shoving the papers aside. *Dad won't be here to
build it. There's no use for the sketch or Ruthie's lumber now.*
Kit sat bolt upright. *Unless . . . wait a minute! Tree house?
Boarding house?*

Suddenly, Kit had an idea.

❉

All through dinner Kit was distracted, thinking about her idea. The more she thought about it, the better she liked it. As soon as they were alone in the kitchen, washing the dishes after dinner, Kit presented her idea to Mother.

"Mother," she said, "I've been thinking. Ruthie's father has a stack of lumber left over from their new garage. He said Ruthie and I could have it to build a tree house. But I bet he wouldn't mind if we used the lumber to fix up Charlie's sleeping porch instead. If we made it nice enough, then maybe Mr. Peck would move in with Charlie."

"And then?" Mother asked.

"Then we could put two new boarders in Mr. Peck's room," said Kit.

"We could certainly use the money," said Mother. She sighed tiredly. "But I just don't know if I could handle the extra work that two more boarders would be." Her face looked sad. "Especially after your father leaves."

"How about asking Mrs. Howard to help you with

the housework instead of paying rent?" asked Kit. "I'd still help, too, of course. But Mrs. Howard is a crackerjack cleaner."

Mother shook her head. "I'm not sure she'd agree to that," she said.

"Oh, I think she would," said Kit. "Stirling says she *wants* to help."

Mother was quiet for a thoughtful moment. Then she said, "Kit, dear, it's very ingenious of you to have thought of all this, and it would be very nice of you and Ruthie to sacrifice your tree house lumber. But I'm afraid lumber for the renovation is not our only problem. We don't have money to pay a carpenter. Who'd do the work?"

Kit sighed and sat down at the kitchen table, discouraged. Then, suddenly, she and Mother looked at each other. They'd both had the same idea at the same time. Together they said, "Dad!"

"Dad could do it!" said Kit. "He's great at building things."

"Yes," agreed Mother. "But the idea would have to be presented to him in just the right way. Now that he's decided to go, it'll be hard to change his mind."

Kit grinned from ear to ear. "You leave that to me," she said, full of enthusiasm. "I have a great plan!"

Mother smiled at last. "All right," she said. "Give it a try!"

"Thanks, Mother!" said Kit. She hugged Mother, and then darted out the kitchen door and flew up the stairs two at a time. She couldn't carry out her plan alone, but she knew just whom to ask for help.

Kit knocked on Stirling's door.

"Yes?" said Mrs. Howard. When she opened the door, Kit saw that the room was as neat as a pin.

"May I please speak to Stirling?" asked Kit.

Mrs. Howard began to say no. "He's very tired, and—"

But then Stirling appeared from behind his mother.

"Stirling," said Kit, looking straight at him. "Will you help me?"

"Yes!" said Stirling immediately. It was as though he'd been waiting for Kit's question for a long time.

❈

The next morning, when Dad sat down to breakfast, this is what he saw at his place:

The Hard Times News

SPECIAL THANKSGIVING DAY EDITION

****

Editor: Kit Kittredge
Artist: Stirling Howard
Adviser: Mother Margaret Kittredge

WANTED

Tall bearded man to share sleeping
porch with early rising, agreeable
teenager. Must play double bass and
drink coffee. Call Charlie Kittredge.

WANTED

Do you have interesting, xexciting stories
to tell about adventures in nursing? If so,
I'd like to hear them! Call Kitt Kittredge.

WANTED IMMEDIATELY

Talented handy man to fix sleeping porch
so that it will sleep two. Great workingg
conditions! Call the Kittredge family.

WANTED

Neat and tidy lady to help with housekeeping in exchange for room and board.
Call Margaret Kittredge..

WANTED

Kids with wagon to haul away any
leftover lumber suitable for use in fixing
sleeping porch. Call Ruthie Smithens.

Kit, Stirling, and Mother sat on the edges of their seats watching Dad read *The Hard Times News*. When he finished reading, Dad glanced at Mother over the top of the paper with a questioning look in his eyes. Mother smiled and nodded, and then Dad smiled, too.

"Well!" said Dad, patting the paper. "Look at this! There's a construction job in these want ads. A boarding house needs to expand. It's right here in Cincinnati, close to home." Dad winked at Kit. "In fact, it *is* at home. It's the perfect job for me!"

Kit ran to Dad and hugged him. "So you'll stay, then?" she asked.

"Yes," said Dad. "I'll go talk to Ruthie's father about the leftover lumber today." He handed Kit's newspaper to Mrs. Howard. "I think there's a job here that might interest you, Mrs. Howard," he said.

Mrs. Howard read the want ads and exclaimed, "My land! So there is!" She turned to Mother. "I'd love to help you with the housekeeping," she said. "I'm very good at dusting. I've noticed that the upstairs hallway—"

"That's Kit's job," Mother interrupted politely. "But with two more boarders moving in soon, there'll be plenty to do. I'd be glad to have your help."

"I'll start today!" said Mrs. Howard.

Kit stood next to Dad and looked around the breakfast table as the newspaper was passed from hand to hand. Charlie and Mr. Peck were laughing and talking together about being roommates. Miss Hart and Miss Finney were beaming at her, looking as if they were brimming over with stories to tell. Suddenly, she heard a quiet voice next to her say, "Happy Thanksgiving, Kit."

It was Stirling. His gray eyes were shining. Kit smiled. "Happy Thanksgiving, Stirling," she said.

Rickrack

fter that, the Kittredges' house seemed more cheerful, more like the home that Kit remembered before Dad lost his job. It was still crowded with boarders, but now the boarders seemed like friends. Thanksgiving *was* a happy day, full of laughter and lively chatter.

But money was still tight. November turned into December, and Dad still hadn't found a job.

On a bright, brisk Saturday afternoon two weeks before Christmas, Kit and Ruthie were cheerfully skittering down the sidewalk together like blown leaves. They were going to the movies, which they loved to do. When the girls were close to the movie theater, Kit leaned forward. She put her fists in her pockets and pushed down so that the front of her coat covered more of her dress.

"Hey, Kit, are you okay?" asked Ruthie kindly. "Does your stomach hurt or something?"

"No," said Kit. "I'm fine."

"Then how come you're all hunched over like that?" asked Ruthie.

"Because," said Kit, "I don't want everyone to see the rickrack on my dress."

"Why not?" asked Ruthie. "It's cute."

"Cute?" said Kit. "I hate it! My mother sewed it over the crease that was left when she let the hem down. I think it looks terrible!" Actually, Kit felt as if the rickrack were a big, embarrassing sign that said to everyone, *Look at this old outgrown dress I have to wear because I'm too poor to get a new one!* But she did not explain that to Ruthie.

Luckily, Ruthie was the kind of friend who was helpful even without explanations. "Walk behind me," she said. "I'll cover you up. Once we're inside the movie theater, it'll be dark and no one will see."

"Okay," said Kit. She scooched up behind Ruthie and the girls went into the theater. It was very warm inside. The air was buttery with the aroma of hot popcorn. And of course Ruthie was right—it *was* dark.

Even so, when Kit sat down, she spread her coat over her lap to hide the rickrack.

"Want some?" asked Ruthie, generously holding out her popcorn to Kit.

"Thanks," said Kit. She took just two pieces of popcorn so that Ruthie wouldn't think she was a moocher. She already felt prickles of guilt because Ruthie had paid for her movie ticket.

Kit didn't see how she'd ever be able to pay Ruthie back. Not that Ruthie expected her to! It just made Kit feel funny to owe money, even to her best friend. Kit squirmed in her seat. It never used to be awkward like this before Dad lost his job. Back then, Kit could pay her fair share. Maybe she shouldn't have agreed today when Ruthie, whose father still had his job at the bank, insisted on paying for her ticket. "Think of it as an early Christmas present," Ruthie had said. *Maybe I shouldn't have given in*, thought Kit.

But as soon as the newsreel began, Kit was very glad she had given in. Because there on the screen, smiling and waving at her, was Kit's absolute heroine— Amelia Earhart! Kit sat on the edge of her seat. The newsreel narrator was saying that Amelia Earhart was the first woman in history to fly a plane across the Atlantic Ocean all by herself. Kit knew everything about that daring solo flight. In fact, Kit had a newspaper article about it tacked to the wall above her desk at home. She'd read it a million times and stared at the photo of Amelia Earhart grinning her cocky, confident grin.

Now Kit stared at the movie screen as Amelia Earhart, in a sporty jacket, flight cap, and gloves, saluted the camera and climbed into the cockpit of her plane. Kit listened to the rumble of the plane's motor. She could almost feel the little plane straining to go faster, faster, faster as Amelia Earhart drove it down the runway. Then at last, she could feel the exhilaration of lifting up off the ground and soaring above the clouds!

The newsreel ended and Kit sank back. But she was so carried away by Amelia Earhart that the cartoon after the newsreel went by her in a blur. When the feature movie began, Kit didn't even try to make sense of the story. It was about a silly woman in a tiara singing and dancing her way up a staircase shaped like a wedding cake.

When at last the movie was over, Kit walked out into the late afternoon sunshine still thinking about

Amelia Earhart. She ignored the rickrack on her skirt hanging out below her old winter coat. Amelia Earhart wouldn't let a thing like that bother *her*.

Ruthie didn't mention the rickrack, either. She turned to Kit and said, "Wasn't she wonderful?"

"Yes!" Kit agreed with enthusiasm. "Thank you so much for bringing me today, Ruthie. I loved watching her climb into that plane, and . . ."

"Not Amelia Earhart," Ruthie laughed. "I meant Dottie Drew, the movie star!"

"Oh, *her*!" said Kit.

"Wasn't she beautiful?" breathed Ruthie. "Like a princess almost."

"Uh, sure!" said Kit. She did not share Ruthie's fascination with movie stars and princesses, but she didn't want to be rude. Ruthie had paid for her ticket, after all. Kit might seem ungrateful if she said she thought the woman in the movie was silly.

But Ruthie knew Kit too well to be fooled. She grinned. "I bet you didn't notice Dottie Drew at all," she said. "I should have known you'd care more about Amelia Earhart. How come you're so crazy about her?"

"She's smart," said Kit. "She's brave, too. When she

makes up her mind to do something, she doesn't let anything stop her. She flew her plane across the ocean all by herself! She didn't need help from anybody." Kit spoke with determination. "I want to be like her."

"I know just what you mean," said Ruthie. "It's the same with me." She sighed. "I love to imagine that I'm a movie star or a princess."

Kit didn't think her serious ambitions were the same as Ruthie's starry-eyed daydreams at all. "That's different, Ruthie," she said. "First of all, Amelia Earhart's a real person who does real things that really matter. Movie stars and princesses are only phony glitter and glamour. And I don't imagine that I *am* Amelia Earhart. I want to be *like* her. Imagining that you're a princess is just make-believe."

"So?" Ruthie shrugged. "There's nothing wrong with make-believe."

"Maybe not," said Kit. "But imaginary stuff doesn't solve any problems or help anything."

"Oh, I think it does," said Ruthie. "Make-believe can take your mind off your troubles for a while. That's a help."

On the sidewalk ahead of the girls, Kit saw a sad

sight. It was a pile of household goods dumped on the curb. A bed frame leaned against a chair, and a lamp lay sideways on the ground. Books, clothes, and pots and pans were jumbled together in a heap. "Look," Kit said to Ruthie, pointing to the pile. "That stuff belongs to a family that's been evicted. They've been thrown out of their house because they can't pay for it anymore. You've got to admit that make-believe and imagination are not going to help *them*."

"They should've imagined a way to get money," Ruthie said. "They could've done *something*."

"I'm sure they tried," said Kit, thinking of how hard her own family struggled to pay the bills every month. "Maybe they just couldn't keep up."

"Then," said Ruthie, "they should have asked their friends for help."

"Maybe they were too proud to do that," said Kit.

Ruthie shook her head sadly. "And look where their pride got them—thrown out on the street," she said. "It won't be a very merry Christmas for their family, will it?"

"No," said Kit. "It won't." She shivered. "Come on," she said to Ruthie. "Let's run. It'll warm us up."

"Last one home is a rotten egg!" said Ruthie.

The girls ran the rest of the way to Kit's house. Kit quickly helped her mother scrub potatoes and put them in the oven before she and Ruthie went upstairs.

The girls were engaged in a secret project with Miss Hart and Miss Finney. The nurses had helped the girls unravel old sweaters and then use the wool to knit scarves. The scarves were almost finished, except for the fringe. Kit and Ruthie planned to give their scarves to their fathers for Christmas. Miss Hart planned to give hers to her boyfriend. Miss Finney said she wasn't sure which lucky guy would get her scarf. She couldn't decide between Tarzan and Franklin Roosevelt, who had just been elected president.

"Any news from Miss Hart's boyfriend lately?" asked Ruthie as the girls walked down the hall.

"Yup," said Kit. "He's coming to Cincinnati at Christmastime."

Miss Hart's boyfriend lived in Boston and sent her long letters in fat envelopes nearly every day. Miss Hart wrote back just as often, and her letters were just as long. Kit and Ruthie were both curious about the letters, and Ruthie especially liked to keep an eye on the progress of Miss Hart's romance.

"Miss Hart must be thrilled," said Ruthie. "Oh, if only they could have a romantic date while he's here! He'd probably ask her to marry him!"

"Miss Hart's boyfriend is a student in medical school," said Kit. "It'll take all his money to travel here. I don't think he'll have any left over for a fancy date."

"I wish he would," said Ruthie dreamily. "Miss Finney and Mr. Peck could go, too, and *they'd* fall in love. That's what would happen if they were in a movie."

"Well," said Kit crisply. "They're not in a movie. They're in real life."

"Too bad," sighed Ruthie.

Kit knocked on the door to Miss Hart and Miss Finney's room. There was no answer. "I guess they're working the weekend shift at the hospital," Kit said. "We won't be able to finish our scarves today. Want to go up to my room and make a newspaper instead?"

"Sure!" said Ruthie with enthusiasm.

"We'll write about Amelia Earhart," said Kit.

"And Dottie Drew!" insisted Ruthie.

Kit pretended to be puzzled. "Who's she?" she asked.

"Very funny," said Ruthie.

"Okay," said Kit, grinning. "Her, too." And she danced up the attic stairs to her room the way Dottie Drew had danced up the wedding cake in the movie.

❀

Ruthie leaned over Kit's shoulder. Kit was typing a paragraph Ruthie had written about Dottie Drew. "Wait a minute," Ruthie said. "It's Dottie Drew, not Duttio Drow. And she's a movie star, not a muvio tar. You better fix those mistakes."

"I can't," sighed Kit. "My typewriter keys are broken. The **o** looks like a **u** and the **e** looks like an **o** and the **s** doesn't work at all."

"Oh, well, that's okay," said Ruthie. She grinned, then said slowly, "I mean . . . uh, woll. That ukay."

Kit grinned, too. "I guess people will figure it out," she said. "Anyway, the pictures are great."

The girls had had the smart idea of asking Stirling to draw sketches of Amelia Earhart and Dottie Drew to illustrate their newspaper. "Stirling's a good artist," said Ruthie as she looked through his sketchpad. "See how he made Amelia Earhart look like you, Kit, freckles and all?"

Kit nodded. "And he put *you* in Dottie Drew's fancy ball gown and tiara," she said.

"That's me. Princess Ruthie," giggled Ruthie, striking a princessly pose.

Kit looked at the paper in her typewriter. "There's still a little space left," she said. "What should we write about?"

"Christmas!" said Ruthie. "We can say, 'Christmas is coming!' Everyone loves to read about that. I personally can't wait. I love everything about Christmas. What's your most favorite part, Kit?"

"Christmas Eve," said Kit. "That's when we put up our tree. Charlie's going to get us a free tree this year. We always decorate our tree on Christmas Eve. It looks so beautiful, especially the lights. We turn them on when we finish decorating, and we have dinner next to the tree. Mother always makes waffles. It's our tradition. I love it."

"I love the tradition that you and I have," said Ruthie, "when we go downtown with our mothers on the day after Christmas."

"Ruthie," Kit began, "I'm sorry. I'm afraid—"

But Ruthie talked over her. "I know you and your

mother are awfully busy this year, what with the
boarding house and all," she said. "So I was thinking
that maybe this Christmas, instead of the whole day,
we could go downtown just for a few hours instead.
That'd be just as fun, wouldn't it?"

Kit believed in telling the truth, even when it was
hard. "Time isn't the only problem, Ruthie," she said.
"My mother and I don't have any money for lunch at
a fancy restaurant or tickets to a show. We don't have
money for presents even. Not this year."

"That's what I figured," said Ruthie. "So I thought
we could change our tradition and just go window-
shopping and have a winter picnic or something."

"I think," said Kit slowly, "it would wreck our tradition to change it."

"We wouldn't change *all* of it," said Ruthie. "We'd
still get all dressed up in our best dresses, and—"

"I'd have to wear this rickrack dress," Kit cut in,
"which I hate." She knew she sounded like a sourpuss,
but she couldn't help it.

"But it's *Christmas*," Ruthie insisted. "You never
know what might happen. You might get a new
dress."

Kit shook her head. "The last thing I want my family to do this Christmas is to spend money on me," she said. "I don't want dresses or outings or presents. The only thing I want is to find a way to make money."

"Find a wicked ogre," said Ruthie. "Lots of times in fairy tales a princess is kind to an ogre, and then he spins straw into gold for her, or he enchants her so that jewels come out of her mouth when she talks, or he grants her three wishes."

Kit felt annoyed at Ruthie and her princesses. She and her family were real people, not characters in a fairy tale. "For Pete's sake!" she said. "It takes work, not wishes, to solve problems. That make-believe stuff is silly. There are no ogres in Cincinnati."

Ruthie just grinned. "Watch out," she said. "If you're not nice, the ogre'll make snakes and toads come out of your mouth. How'd you like that?"

"Not much," said Kit. Impatiently, she pushed the silver arm that moved the paper up and out of the typewriter. But she pushed a little too hard, because, to her horror, it came off in her hand. "Oh no!" she cried, holding the silver arm up for Ruthie to see. "Look what I've done!"

"Uh-oh," said Ruthie. "Can you screw it back on?"

"No!" said Kit. "Oh, now the typewriter won't work at all!"

"Come on," said Ruthie, heading for the stairs. "Let's go get your dad. I bet he can fix it."

"I sure hope so," said Kit.

The two girls hurried downstairs. They paused in the hallway outside the living room because they heard Kit's parents talking to someone. The conversation sounded serious, so they knew they shouldn't barge in and interrupt.

Kit's dad was talking. "The room should be ready by the middle of January," he said. "Then we can take in two more boarders."

"I'm afraid that'll be too late," said the other voice. The girls looked at each other in surprise. It was Ruthie's dad, Mr. Smithens, speaking. Ruthie started to go into the room, but Kit held her back. "I've come today as a friend," Mr. Smithens said. "Your name is on a list of people who owe money to the bank, people who're behind on their mortgage payments. I came to warn you that if you can't catch up on your payments, the bank will take your house and you'll be evicted."

Evicted! Kit felt as if she'd been punched in the stomach.

"I'll hold off the bank until after the holidays," Ruthie's dad said. "But if you can borrow the money from someone, you should. Do you think your aunt in Kentucky might help, Jack? Or, Margaret, how about your uncle here in Cincinnati?"

Kit's mother started to answer, saying, "Well, I—"

"Thanks, Stan," Kit's dad interrupted. "We'll figure something out."

Kit could hardly breathe. Evicted! She and her family were going to be thrown out of their house! All of their belongings would be tossed out onto the sidewalk, just like those she and Ruthie had seen on their way home from the movies. *It's going to happen to my family*, she thought. *It's going to happen to me.* She shuddered, and Ruthie touched her arm.

"Oh, Kit," Ruthie whispered. "What'll you do? I wish . . ."

Wish! thought Kit. She jerked her arm away. She couldn't bear to hear Ruthie say one of her silly things about wishes and princesses and make-believe. Not now. It was bad enough that Ruthie had been there to overhear the terrible, humiliating news! Without a word, Kit turned sharply and went back up the stairs to her room, leaving Ruthie all alone in the hall.

The Bright Red Dress

❀ CHAPTER 10 ❀

That night, after the last dinner dish was washed and dried, Mother took off her apron, put on her hat and coat, and went out. She didn't say where she was going, but Kit knew. Mother was paying a visit to Uncle Hendrick, who lived alone in a big, gloomy house near downtown Cincinnati. Kit knew Mother was going to ask Uncle Hendrick for money so that they wouldn't be evicted from their house.

Kit was reading in bed when Mother returned. When she came up to kiss Kit good night, Mother's face was tired.

"Uncle Hendrick said no, didn't he?" said Kit.

Mother was surprised. "How did—" she began.

"I heard Mr. Smithens talking to you and Dad," Kit said in her straightforward way. "I know about us being evicted. I figured you went to Uncle Hendrick to ask for money. And," Kit repeated, "he said no, didn't he?"

"I'm sorry, Kit," Mother said sadly. "It's not fair for a child to have to worry about such things." She sighed. "But you're right. Uncle Hendrick believes that money must be earned by hard work, not given away. He says we've been living beyond our means. He thinks it was foolish of us to buy this big house in the first place, and it would be throwing good money after bad to help us keep it. If we are evicted, he wants us to move in with him."

Kit sat bolt upright. "Oh, no!" she said. "We'd hate that! All the boarders would leave. It'd be awful."

Mother smiled a sad smile. "We may not have a choice," she said. "And we may lose the boarders anyway. At this point, we don't have enough money to pay even the electric bill. I don't think we can ask the boarders to stay if our electricity is cut off and we don't have any lights."

Kit couldn't bear to see Mother look so defeated. "I'll find a way to help, Mother," she said. "I promise I will. I'll find a way to make money."

"Well," said Mother, "there is a way you can help,

though I don't think it'll make any money."

"What is it?" asked Kit.

"Uncle Hendrick says he's ill," said Mother. "I think he's really just lonely and fretful. But he wants me to come back tomorrow and every day until he feels better. I'm so busy here, I don't see how I can. Would you do it? You could go tomorrow, and then next week you could go after school. During your Christmas vacation, you could go for a few hours every day. He needs someone to keep him company and do errands and walk his dog."

Kit's heart sank. Uncle Hendrick's old black Scottie dog, Inky, was the meanest, most hateful dog in Cincinnati. He was even meaner than Uncle Hendrick. And Uncle Hendrick was exactly like Ebenezer Scrooge in *A Christmas Carol* before the ghosts visited him and scared him into being nice. "I know it's a lot to ask," said Mother. "But it would be a great help to me."

"I'll do it," said Kit. This was her chance to help.

Mother hugged Kit. "That's my girl," she said, and now her smile was real. "Thank you. Uncle Hendrick knows we don't have a car anymore. He gave me a nickel for the streetcar. I'll give it to you tomorrow.

Now don't read too long. You need to rest. Good night!"

"Good night!" said Kit.

Mother went downstairs. Kit had read only a few pages when her brother Charlie appeared. "Hi," he said. "Mother told me what you're doing. I thought you could use this." He tossed an old tennis ball to Kit.

"What's this for?" she asked as she caught it.

"It's for stinky Inky to fetch," said Charlie. "Throw it really, *really* far."

Kit grinned. "Thanks, Charlie," she said.

Charlie grinned, too. "You're welcome," he said. "G'night, Squirt!"

"'Night, Charlie!" said Kit. She switched off her light and lay in the dark thinking, *Maybe Uncle Hendrick's won't be so bad after all.*

❈

But it *was* bad. In fact, it was terrible.

The first bad thing that happened was that Kit missed the streetcar. She had to run all the way to Uncle Hendrick's house because she was supposed to be there promptly at noon and Uncle Hendrick was a stickler for time. Luckily, Kit was a fast runner. But it was very cold, and Kit's nose was red and her hair was blown every which way by the time she got to Uncle Hendrick's door. She tried to catch her breath and straighten herself up a little. But Inky was barking wildly and scrabbling his claws against the other side of the door, so Uncle Hendrick opened it before she even knocked. That was the next bad thing.

"What are *you* doing here?" he bellowed over Inky's yapping.

"Mother's too busy," Kit bellowed back. "I'm here instead."

"I don't want *you*," said Uncle Hendrick. "Go away!"

Inky growled as if to echo Uncle Hendrick, then launched into another frenzy of barking.

Kit didn't budge. She'd promised Mother that she would help. It would take more than Uncle Hendrick's bluster and Inky's snarls to discourage her.

"Well, you're here, so you might as well stay," said Uncle Hendrick. "Hurry up! Come in! Don't stand there like a fool and let the heat out. It costs good money." Kit stepped inside, and he shut the door behind her. "If your family had paid more attention to how much

things like heat cost, you wouldn't be in the state you're
in now," he scolded. "Come with me."

"Yes, sir," said Kit. Now that the door was shut,
she realized how dark it was inside Uncle Hendrick's
house. The darkness seemed old somehow, and permanent, as if it had been there a long time and always
would be there. Kit followed Uncle Hendrick and Inky
upstairs to Uncle Hendrick's huge room. He sat down
in the most comfortable chair by the coal fire and put a
blanket over his knees. Inky jumped up into the other
chair by the fire. He watched Kit's every move with his
sharp, unfriendly black eyes.

Kit went to Uncle Hendrick to give him the nickel
she hadn't used.

"What's that?" he snapped, peering at the coin.

"It's the nickel you gave Mother for the streetcar,"
said Kit. "I didn't use it. I missed the streetcar, so I—"

"I don't care if you came on a winged chariot,"
Uncle Hendrick said, impatiently pushing her hand
away. "You got here on time. That's all that matters."

"You mean I can keep the nickel?" asked Kit.

"Yes!" barked Uncle Hendrick, sounding a lot like
Inky. "Now stop jabbering! Hand me my book! Not

the red one, the brown one! And how am I supposed
to read it? Hand me my eyeglasses, too, and be quick
about it."

That's how it went all afternoon. Uncle Hendrick
sat in his chair and ordered Kit downstairs to make
him a cup of tea. When she brought it up, he ordered
her downstairs again for the milk and sugar. He
wanted her to open the drapes, then close them again,
to move his chair closer to the fire and then farther
away. He wanted his medicine. He wanted the newspaper. He wanted a pen and ink and writing paper,
then a stamp.

It seemed to Kit that for an old man who was supposed to be sick, Uncle Hendrick certainly had plenty
of energy for bossing her around and pointing out
what she was doing wrong, which was everything. She
filled the teacup too full and sloshed tea into the saucer.
She wobbled the spoon when she poured the medicine
into it. She pulled too hard on the cord that closed the
drapes but didn't push hard enough when moving his
chair. She talked too fast and walked too slow. There
was no pleasing Uncle Hendrick.

Inky was just as bad. When it was time for his

walk, Kit put her coat back on. She clipped Inky's leash onto his collar. "Come, Inky," she said. Inky didn't move. He growled deep in his throat and bared his teeth at her.

"You'll have to carry him," said Uncle Hendrick. "He doesn't like walking down the stairs."

Kit hoisted the fat old dog up in her arms and carried him down the stairs and out the door. Once his feet hit the sidewalk, Inky took off. He strained on the leash, practically pulling Kit's arm out of its socket. When they got to the park, Kit bent down to show Inky the tennis ball. "Look, Inky," she said. Then she threw the ball as hard as she could. "Go get it, Inky!" she said.

But Inky just sniffed, as if to say, "Why should I?" He lowered himself to the grass and refused to move. Kit had to fetch the ball herself, and then drag Inky back to Uncle Hendrick's house and carry him upstairs.

"You," she hissed, as she set him down, "are a horrible dog."

Inky's black eyes glittered. He looked pleased with himself. He jumped into his chair and promptly went to sleep.

Uncle Hendrick was asleep, too. So Kit had to sit perfectly still and wait for him to wake up. She amused herself by thinking of words to describe Uncle Hendrick and Inky. *They're both grouchy and grumpy,* she thought. *They're crabby, cranky, critical, and cross.*

When at last Uncle Hendrick woke up, he announced that it was time for Kit to go home. Kit put on her coat, which was now covered with Inky's black hair. "Good-bye," she said to Uncle Hendrick. "I'll see you tomorrow."

"Humph," said Uncle Hendrick. He didn't sound pleased or displeased. He reached into his pocket and pulled out two nickels. "Here," he said. "One for the streetcar home and one for the streetcar here tomorrow."

"But—" Kit began to say.

"Take them and go!" ordered Uncle Hendrick.

So she did.

When she closed the door behind her, Kit took a deep breath. The cold, clean winter air felt wonderful on her cheeks. It cleared the stuffy, mediciney, doggy smell of Uncle Hendrick's house out of her nose. As Kit walked to the streetcar stop, she had an idea.

I'll walk home, she thought. *Uncle Hendrick said he*

didn't care if I use the nickels for the streetcar or not. I won't use them. I'll save them and give them to Mother to help pay the electric bill. That will be my Christmas surprise for her.

The thought cheered Kit, and she turned up her collar and started the long walk home with determined steps. But it was awfully cold, and the walk was all uphill. By the time Kit got to her own house, she was tired and cold to the bone. She was hungry, too. It was disheartening to know she had missed Sunday dinner and there'd be only crackers and milk for supper.

When Kit opened the front door, she was surprised to see Ruthie sitting on the bottom step in the front hall. Ruthie had a big white box on her lap. Her face was bright and eager. She looked as if she was struggling to hold a surprise inside and was about to burst. "Hi!" she said to Kit. "I thought you'd never get here!"

"Hi," said Kit as she wearily hung up her coat. "I don't think we can finish our scarves today, Ruthie. I have chores to do."

"Oh, I didn't come for that!" said Ruthie. She jumped up from the stair and thrust the big white box at Kit. "Here!" she said. "This is for you." Ruthie was so excited, she danced around Kit impatiently as Kit knelt down to open the box. "Wait till you see!" she said. "Now everything will be okay!"

Kit lifted the lid of the box. Inside, she saw a bright red dress. She took it out and held it up, puzzled. "But this is your dress, Ruthie," she said at last.

"It *was*," said Ruthie. "It's my last year's Christmas dress. It doesn't fit me anymore. I'm getting a new one, so I'm giving this one to you."

The bright red dress was *so* red it seemed to make Kit's hands warm just to hold it. Kit felt her face get warm, too, but the heat came from the burning sting of embarrassment. She was humiliated, not delighted, by Ruthie's hand-me-down present. *Now Ruthie thinks of me as a poor, pitiful beggar girl,* she thought. Kit swallowed. "Thanks," she managed to say politely. She tried very hard to smile.

"That's not all!" Ruthie burbled. "Look in the pocket! It's even better."

Kit reached into the pocket of the dress and pulled out four tickets to the ballet. There was also an invitation in Ruthie's handwriting that said:

Mrs. Smithens and Ruthie Smithens
cordially invite
Mrs. Kittredge and Kit Kittredge
to a fancy tea at
Shillito's Restaurant
on December 26th
after the ballet

"See?" said Ruthie, all aglow. "My mother bought the tickets, and she'll pay for the tea. Now we *can* have our special day. And you won't have to wear your rick-rack dress."

Slowly, Kit slid the invitation and the tickets back into the pocket. She folded the dress carefully and put the lid back on the box. She stood up. "Thank you, Ruthie," she said stiffly. "But your dress is probably too big for me. And my mother and I are going to be busy on December 26th." She handed the big white box to Ruthie.

Ruthie looked at it, then at Kit. "What do you mean?" she asked.

"I have a job now," said Kit. "At my Uncle Hendrick's house."

"But you could take a day off," said Ruthie. "You could—"

"No," interrupted Kit coolly. "I couldn't. It's my responsibility." Ruthie's face looked so sad that Kit softened a bit. "Listen," she said. "I know you're just trying to be nice and generous, Ruthie. But don't you see? I can't wear your old dress."

"But my mother fixed it to fit you," said Ruthie. "And I thought you were embarrassed by the rickrack dress. I thought you hated it."

"I do hate it," said Kit. "But at least it's my own. I'd be embarrassed to wear your dress. And it's the same with the tickets and the tea. It would make my mother and me feel like sponges."

"Sponges?" asked Ruthie. Her voice sounded strained and tight.

"Yes," said Kit. "We'd be ashamed to let your mother pay for us."

"Ashamed!" said Ruthie, pink in the face and mad. "I think you should be ashamed of being so selfish. You're just only thinking of yourself! What about me?

Did you ever stop to think that maybe you're ruining my Christmas with your stupid pride? You've got a houseful of people, and I'm all alone with just my mother and father. The most fun I ever have is with you. The day you and I spend together after Christmas is the very best part of Christmas for me. I thought you liked it, too. That's why my mother and I tried to fix it this year. But you're too stuck-up and stubborn to accept it. We were just trying to help."

"I don't want help," said Kit, bristling.

"Oh, I know!" said Ruthie. "You think you're just like great old Amelia Earhart, flying all by herself without help from anybody."

Now Kit was mad, too. "At least I'm not so babyish that I think I'm a princess like you do," she said, the words lashing out as mean as snakes. "You're always talking about wishes and wicked ogres and make-believe. You don't know anything that's real. Your father still has his job. You can do whatever you want. You have everything, except you don't have any idea what the world is really like!"

"Well, now I know what *you* are really like," said Ruthie. "Mean."

"Well, you're spoiled," said Kit.

"Oh!" exclaimed Ruthie angrily. She grabbed her coat and went to the door. "I don't think we can be friends anymore."

"Good!" said Kit.

"Good-*bye*!" said Ruthie. Then she left, closing the door firmly behind her.

Kit stared at the door for a second, then turned and ran as fast as she could up the stairs to her room. She flung herself face-down on her bed. Oh, oh, *oh!* How could everything be so horrible? It wasn't *fair*. Her family had lost so much since Dad had lost his job. Not just money. They'd lost their feeling of being safe, their trust that things would work out for the best. They were probably going to lose their home. *And now I've lost the most important thing of all*, thought Kit. *My best friend*.

Kit buried her face in her pillow and cried.

The Wicked Ogre

Kit couldn't allow herself to cry for long. She knew that all her afternoon chores were waiting for her. And Mother liked to give the kitchen floor a good scrub every Sunday night because there wasn't time during the week. Kit rolled over and sat up on her bed. She saw Amelia Earhart smiling at her from the newspaper photograph near her desk. *Come on, Kit,* Amelia seemed to say. *Gotta get up and go.* Even though she still felt miserable, Kit wiped her eyes, blew her nose, and went downstairs to the kitchen.

Mother had already put the chairs up on the kitchen table. She was filling a bucket with hot, soapy water at the sink. She turned to greet Kit with a smile. But her smile faded when she saw Kit's eyes, red from crying. "Oh, Kit, darling!" she said. She dried her hands on her apron as she hurried over to put her arm around Kit. "Was it that bad at Uncle Hendrick's, then? He's so fussy. And that awful what's-his-name, too. The Scottie dog!"

"Inky," Kit said. Mother smelled of soapsuds, and Kit let herself lean against her. "He hates me."

"The way to that dog's heart is through his stomach," said Mother. "I've got some cheese rinds in the pantry. Even I can't figure out how to make them edible. You can give them to Inky tomorrow when you go there after school. That'll win him over."

"Thanks, Mother," said Kit, not very cheered.

"That's not all that's wrong, is it?" asked Mother.

"No," admitted Kit. "Ruthie and I had a fight."

"I see," said Mother. "What about?"

Kit poured out the whole story about Ruthie's bright red dress, the ballet tickets, and the invitation to tea. "It was wrong of me to say no for you, too," she said. "But I couldn't help it. I was just so *mad*." Kit sighed. "It used to be easy to be friends with Ruthie. It isn't anymore."

Mother nodded. "Your lives are very different now," she said. "Things that are possible for Ruthie are not possible for you."

"The truth is," said Kit, "I'm jealous of her."

"And she," said Mother, "is jealous of you."

"Of me?" asked Kit, surprised. "But I'm the one who's lost everything. Why would she be jealous of me?"

"Oh, I don't know," said Mother. "I've had the impression that Ruthie envies you for having the boarders around, like a big, interesting family. It's awfully quiet at her house. And maybe she envies how your life is more grown-up now. People trust you to do important things."

"I never thought of it that way," said Kit, sighing. "All I know is that I'm sorry about the fight."

"I wish we could use the telephone," said Mother. The telephone had been turned off because they couldn't afford to pay the bill anymore. "Then you could call Ruthie and tell her that you're sorry. Well, you'll see her in school tomorrow. You can make it better then."

"Do you think so?" asked Kit hopefully.

"Of course!" said Mother. "It is never too late to repair a friendship." Mother lifted the pail of hot water out of the sink. "Let's scrub this floor now," she said. "I'm afraid it's never too late for that, either!"

❄

Mother was wrong. Kit was not able to patch
things up with Ruthie the next day. Ruthie didn't stop
to pick her up before school. And every time Kit tried
to get Ruthie's attention during the morning, Ruthie
turned away or hid herself in a group of girls. At
lunchtime, in desperation, Kit wrote Ruthie a note and
put it on her desk. She watched unhappily as Ruthie
glanced at it, picked it up in two fingers as if it were a
dead toad, and tossed it, unopened and unread, into
the wastepaper basket. Then Ruthie sashayed off to
lunch with a bunch of girls who were in her dancing
class. Kit used to be in the dancing class, too, but she'd
had to drop out when her family couldn't afford *that*
anymore, either.

Everyone at school noticed that Ruthie was shun-
ning Kit. Stirling, who was actually pretty nice for a
boy, tried to help. "Here," he said to Kit. "Give this to
Ruthie." He handed Kit a picture he had drawn. The
picture showed Kit flying an airplane like Amelia
Earhart's. The passenger in the airplane was Ruthie
dressed as a princess.

"Thanks, Stirling," Kit said. But she was afraid to
give the drawing to Ruthie after what she'd said about

princesses being babyish. So Kit put Stirling's drawing away in her book bag.

After three days of getting the cold shoulder, Kit gave up. It was clear that Ruthie was too mad to forgive her. She wouldn't even give Kit a chance to apologize. When Ruthie had said they couldn't be friends anymore, she'd meant it. School closed for vacation, and Kit and Ruthie still hadn't spoken.

Usually, Kit loved Christmas vacation because it meant she had more time to spend with her family and Ruthie. But this year, all it meant was that she had more time to spend with Uncle Hendrick and Inky. Uncle Hendrick still claimed he felt poorly, so every morning, after doing her chores at home, Kit went to his house. She walked there and back so she could save the streetcar fare. Her pile of nickels was growing. But that was the only good thing about going to Uncle Hendrick's house.

"Good gracious, you careless child! Don't use so much string!" Uncle Hendrick fussed at her one day as Kit was tying up a bundle of newspapers for him. "Do you think string grows on trees? I suppose you learned your wasteful ways from your spendthrift parents." He snorted. "They think that *money* grows on trees. Holes in their pockets, those two!"

Kit bit her lip to stop herself from saying to Uncle Hendrick, "That's not true!" He never missed a chance to be critical of her parents. He lectured her about how they deserved their poverty because they'd been extravagant and lived beyond their means. It made Kit furious. Sometimes she thought Uncle Hendrick was trying to make her mad on purpose so that she wouldn't come back. But Kit could be ornery, too. The meaner Uncle Hendrick was, the more determined she was not to give up. She wouldn't give him that satisfaction.

At the end of every day, Uncle Hendrick had errands for her to do on her way home. Every errand came with lots of fussbudgety instructions. "Take these shoes to be shined," Uncle Hendrick commanded one blustery day. "Here's a dime to pay for it." He shook his finger at Kit. "Tell the man that I demand good value for my money. The last time, he left a scuff mark on the toe. Tell him don't think I didn't see it."

"Yes, sir," said Kit. She put the shoes in her book bag and the dime in her pocket.

"Leave these shirts at the laundry," said Uncle Hendrick. "Tell them to put starch on the collars and cuffs *only*. And tell them that I don't want to see any buttons broken like the last time or I'll deduct the cost of the buttons from their bill."

"Yes, sir," said Kit again. "Good-bye." She gathered up the shirts, put on her coat, and left.

The laundry was closest, so Kit dropped off the shirts first. Then she trudged along to the shoe-shine shop. When she got there, a terrible sight met her eyes. There was a big hand-lettered sign on the door that said, "OUT OF BUSINESS. Closed till the Depression is Out of Business, too!"

Kit stood there in the bitter cold wondering what to do. One thing was sure. Uncle Hendrick would bite her head off and howl worse than Inky if she brought his shoes back unshined. So Kit took the shoes home. Using her dad's rags and polish, she shined them herself, rubbing until her arm ached. She carried the shoes back to Uncle Hendrick's house the next day, bracing herself for his persnickety words of criticism.

Before she could explain, Uncle Hendrick took the shoes from her. "There!" he said. "That's what I call a job well-done! Let that be a lesson to you, Kit. You only get your money's worth if you insist upon it."

Kit hid a smile. "Here's your dime back," she said. "The shop was closed. I shined the shoes."

"You?" said Uncle Hendrick. He studied the shoes again, then narrowed his eyes at her. "Then you earned the dime," he said brusquely. "Keep it."

Kit put the dime in her pocket. Then she faced Uncle Hendrick bravely. "Uncle Hendrick," she said. "I've been thinking. May I work for you? If I pick up your groceries, may I keep the tip you usually give the delivery man? If I deliver your letters, may I keep the cost of the stamps? And if I—"

"Stop!" shouted Uncle Hendrick. "You pester the life out of me! Get this straight once and for all, child. I don't care who does the work, as long as it's done to my satisfaction. You may keep any money you earn. Understand?"

"Yes, sir!" said Kit.

"Good!" said Uncle Hendrick. "Now don't bother me about this again."

That was all Kit needed to hear.

Starting then, whenever she could, Kit did Uncle Hendrick's jobs herself. She polished his shoes. She

delivered his letters. She fetched his groceries. She
brought him his newspaper. She washed his windows—and then washed them all over again because
Uncle Hendrick said he saw streaks. Kit wanted to earn
enough money to pay the electric bill, which she knew
was about two dollars and thirty-five cents. Every day,
she counted up the money she'd earned to see how
close she was getting to her goal. Five days before
Christmas Eve, Kit had one dollar and fifty-five cents.
She needed eighty cents more. She knew she could earn
ten cents a day by walking instead of riding the streetcar. That would be fifty cents. But it was going to be
tough to earn the last thirty cents.

Still, Kit was determined, even though Uncle
Hendrick's chores were hard. The winter streets were
often slippery, and the winter darkness came earlier
and earlier. But Kit kept saying to herself, *Think how
surprised Mother will be when I give her the money I've
earned.* The thought kept her going when the cold wind
made her eyes water and slush seeped through her
shoes and froze her feet. Sometimes Kit had to take
dreadful old Inky with her when she did errands. He'd
wind his leash around her legs and try to trip her, or

roll in a puddle and then shake so that cold, dirty water splattered all over her. The *clink* of coins in her pocket helped Kit put up with Inky, and with Uncle Hendrick, too, even when he was at his most cantankerous.

There was one errand Kit liked to do even though it didn't earn her any money. Every few days, Uncle Hendrick sent her to the public library to return his books and pick up new ones the librarian set aside for him. The huge public library seemed like a hushed, warm heaven to Kit, filled as it was from floor to ceiling with books. Unfortunately, she never had time to linger there. Uncle Hendrick was always in a hurry to get his books, which seemed odd because they were so dull and boring they always put him to sleep.

It was during the afternoons while Uncle Hendrick dozed that Kit thought about Ruthie the most. She missed Ruthie. It would have been such a comfort to talk to her. She'd understand how hateful Inky was and how impossible Uncle Hendrick was.

One especially long afternoon, Kit sat watching Uncle Hendrick snore in his chair. One of his dull books had put him to sleep. Inky was contentedly tearing the cover off Charlie's tennis ball. Kit reached into her book bag, only to find that she'd left the book she wanted to read at home. Instead, she pulled out a pad of paper. It was Stirling's sketchpad, the one he'd used when he made sketches of Kit as Amelia Earhart and Ruthie as a princess. Kit looked at the sketches. Then, without planning to, she began to write.

Once upon a time, she began. And then the story seemed to sweep her away. It wasn't the kind of story she usually wrote for her newspaper. This story was not about facts. It didn't report what was really happening. This story was about a completely different world, the kind of world Ruthie liked, a world that was imaginary. In this world, Kit could make anything she wanted to happen *happen.*

While she was writing, Kit forgot she was stuck in Uncle Hendrick's dreary house. She forgot about her family's money troubles, and the fact that the boarders might leave, and that her family might be evicted from their house. All that disappeared while she was in the world of her story.

When Uncle Hendrick woke up and blinked his eyes open, Kit felt herself snap back into the real world. It was as if she were waking up, too, from a wonderful dream. Kit hurriedly shoved the sketchpad back into her book bag, thinking, *Ruthie was right! Make-believe does make your troubles disappear for a while.* Kit wished she could tell Ruthie that she understood about make-believe now. Then Kit remembered that she and Ruthie weren't friends anymore. They weren't even speaking to each other.

After that first afternoon, Kit wrote more of her story every day. She began to look forward to her writing time, when the only sounds in the grim old house were Uncle Hendrick's snores, the hollow ticking of the clock on the mantel, and Inky's slobbery snuffles. Soon Kit began to see that writing made *all* of her day better. She thought about her story when she was outside doing errands, and it distracted her from the cold and her tired feet. She paid close attention to how things looked or smelled or sounded, trying to find just the right words to describe them for her story. When Uncle Hendrick woke up and fussed at her, it didn't bother her anymore. She listened carefully, in case she wanted to use anything he said in her story. Because Kit had discovered that Ruthie had been right about something else, too. There *was* a wicked ogre in Cincinnati: Uncle Hendrick.

Jewels

❊ CHAPTER 12 ❊

hooosh!

WA harsh wind blew sleet into Kit's face.
She hunched her shoulders and wrapped
her arms tightly around Uncle Hendrick's library books
to keep them dry. It was Christmas Eve morning, and
even a long list of errands and nasty weather could not
dampen Kit's spirits. *I bet this sleet will turn into snow!*
she thought. *How perfect! It'll be so cozy to have dinner
next to the Christmas tree.*

Kit's family had not had time to put up their Christmas tree yet. But Kit was not worried. As soon as she
was finished at Uncle Hendrick's this afternoon, she'd
hurry home and help Dad and Charlie put up the tree
and decorate it. Kit skipped with happiness, thinking
of how surprised everyone would be when she gave
Mother the money she had earned. Two dollars and

forty cents—enough to pay the electric bill! She had earned the last thirty-five cents by selling Uncle Hendrick's rags to the ragman. *Now the boarders won't leave,* she thought. *Now we can light the Christmas tree lights and our tree will be as beautiful as every other year.*

Kit let herself into Uncle Hendrick's house. Inky barked at her as she climbed the stairs, and nipped at her feet as she went into Uncle Hendrick's room. "Stop that, Inky," said Kit. But the irritating dog would not settle down. He was restless all morning, prowling from window to window. Whenever the sleet clattered against the glass, sounding like a handful of thrown pebbles, Inky barked. Every once in a while, there'd be a loud *CRACK!* when a tree limb, weighted down by a heavy coating of ice, would snap. Inky howled whenever that happened.

When it was time for Inky's walk after lunch, the sleet still hadn't turned to snow. The dog stubbornly refused to go out, so Kit had to carry him, squirming and yowling, out the back door. "Go ahead and yowl," she said to him. "Even you can't ruin this day for me, you horrible dog." She shivered as she waited for Inky to come back inside. It was bitterly cold, and the sleet showed no signs of stopping. Kit rubbed her arms with her hands. She tilted her head to look at the sky. It looked gray and hard, as if it, too, were encased in ice.

At last it was time for Kit to go home. She hurried into her coat and put her book bag on her back. She knew it was going to be a difficult and slippery walk home, and she was anxious to get started. "Good-bye," she said to Uncle Hendrick. "We'll see you tomorrow." Uncle Hendrick was much better, so he planned to take a cab to the Kittredges' house for Christmas Day.

"What? Oh! Yes, of course," said Uncle Hendrick. "Go along now. And close the door carefully behind you. I don't want it banging in this wind."

"Yes, sir!" said Kit. Joyfully, she pounded down the stairs and opened the door. A cruel blast of wind pushed so hard against her that she stumbled back. She bent her head forward, burying her chin in her collar, and pulled the door closed behind her. Ice slashed at her cheeks and stung her eyes. The streetlights were lit, and the street looked eerily beautiful. The tree branches were shiny with ice and glittered as if they were made of diamonds.

Kit took a step forward, and her feet flew out from

under her. She landed hard on her bottom, so hard
that she saw stars. Gingerly, Kit rolled to her hands
and knees and tried to stand. She clutched at the iron
railing that fenced Uncle Hendrick's yard, and inched
her way forward to the sidewalk. It was slow going,
and when the iron railing ended and there was nothing
to hold on to, Kit fell again. This time she cracked her
elbow so badly she winced with pain. Kit blinked back
tears. She struggled to her feet again and tried to skate
forward. But it was no use. For every step forward she
managed to take, she seemed to slip backward twice
as far. If she couldn't make any headway on the flat
ground, there was no way she could get up the steep
hill home, or even to the streetcar stop. Kit's coat was
beaded with pearls of ice, and ice trickled down the
back of her neck. Her feet were so numb they were
heavy as lead. Sadly, Kit fought her way back to Uncle
Hendrick's house and let herself inside.

"What are you doing here?" Uncle Hendrick
snapped when he saw her.

"It's too slippery out," said Kit. "May I wait here till
the sleet stops?"

Uncle Hendrick peered out the window. "It's not going to stop tonight," he announced, sounding pleased to give such bad news. "You'll have to stay the night."

"Oh *no!*" wailed Kit. "I can't. It's Christmas Eve. I *have* to get home."

"Don't be ridiculous!" barked Uncle Hendrick. "Stop whining! There's nothing to be done. You'll have to call your family and tell them you're staying here tonight."

"I can't," said Kit.

"Why not?" asked Uncle Hendrick impatiently.

"Our phone's not connected anymore," said Kit.

"Couldn't pay the bill, I suppose," said Uncle Hendrick sourly. "Typical! Well, then you'll have to call someone who can go to your house to tell your parents where you are. Call a neighbor or a friend."

A friend? Now Kit's heart felt as heavy and leaden as her feet. There was only one person she could call, and that was the last person on earth she wanted to call. But Kit had no choice. She went to the phone. Reluctantly, she made the call. *Maybe her mother will answer,* she thought.

But no. When the voice on the other end of the line said hello, Kit knew who it was right away.

"Ruthie?" she said. "It's me." Kit spoke all in a rush. "I know you're mad at me, but don't hang up. You don't have to talk to me. I wouldn't have called, but I'm stuck at my Uncle Hendrick's house. It's too icy and I can't get home. I need you to tell my parents I'm spending the night at Uncle Hendrick's. Okay?"

There was a pause. "Okay," said Ruthie. She sounded very far away.

"Wait, Ruthie!" said Kit. "One more thing. I . . . I wanted to say I'm sorry. I'm really sorry."

The line got all crackly and Inky started to bark and jump up on Kit, so she couldn't hear if Ruthie said anything or not. Finally, Kit hung up.

❈

The room Kit was supposed to sleep in was as cold as a tomb and about as cheery. It had brown wallpaper. The bed was huge, with a headboard that had wooden gargoyles carved into it. The blankets were mustard-colored and musty-smelling. They were heavy, but somehow they didn't keep Kit warm, even though she pulled them up to her nose. No coal fire had been lit in the fireplace for a long, long time. *If we are evicted from our house, and we have to come and live with Uncle Hendrick, will this be my room?* Kit wondered. She shuddered. *I'd rather live in a dungeon.*

For endless hours, Kit lay stiff and miserable, listening to the ice pelt against the window and the wind rage and the house creak and shift. She thought about all that she was missing at home. By now they would have finished decorating the tree. It probably looked very nice, though most likely Dad wouldn't have put any lights on it. He didn't know they were going to be able to pay the electric bill. He didn't know about Kit's surprise. A lump rose in Kit's throat.

Just then, she heard scratching at her door. Kit hid her head under the covers. But it was no use. The scratching only grew louder, and now Kit heard whimpering, too. She tiptoed across the freezing floor and opened the door a crack. Suddenly, something pushed against it. A dark streak bolted across the floor and leaped up onto her bed. It was Inky. Kit climbed back into bed, and Inky curled up next to her. *This has got to be the worst Christmas Eve anyone has ever had!* Kit thought. *No one deserves a Christmas Eve as lonely as this. Not even Inky.* Kit felt so forlorn, she was actually glad

for horrible old Inky's smelly, snuffling company. At
least he was warm. After a while, Kit fell asleep.

It seemed as if no time at all had passed before a
sound woke her. It was the most peculiar thing. Kit
was sure she heard jingle bells. She opened her eyes
and realized it was morning. The light in the room was
murky because of the heavy curtains drawn shut in
front of the window. Kit got up and pulled the curtains
open. Suddenly, the room was flooded with dazzling
light. The sun, shining on the dripping, melting ice
outside, made prisms of light swim and shimmer on
the walls. The sound of the jingle bells was louder. Kit
looked out the window, squinting because the bright
light was so blinding. She blinked. She couldn't believe
what she saw outside on the sidewalk.

Ruthie and Ruthie's father were standing next to
their big black car, jingling bells and looking up at the
house.

"Ho, ho, ho! Merry Christmas!" shouted Ruthie
when she saw Kit's face at the window. "We've come to
rescue you! Hurry up and come down!"

Kit rose up on her toes in happiness. She banged
on the window. "I'll be right there!" she yelled. She'd

slept in her clothes, so all she had to do was yank on
her shoes, which she did, hopping on one foot and then
the other, before she dashed down the stairs. She flung
open the door and ran straight to Ruthie. "Oh, Ruthie!"
she said. "I've never been so happy to see anyone in my
life! Thank you for helping me!"

Ruthie smiled. "That's what friends are for," she
said.

Kit smiled, too. *Friends!* she thought happily.

When Uncle Hendrick was ready, Mr. Smithens
drove them all—including Inky—to the Kittredges'
house. Though most of the ice had melted, the roads
were slippery, and it was slow going up the hill. Mr.
Smithens skidded as he turned into the Kittredges'
driveway, but he pulled the car as close to the house as
possible. The front door flew open. Mother, Dad, Charlie, and all the boarders poured out calling, "Hurray!"
and "Merry Christmas!" and "Kit, we missed you!"
When Kit jumped out of the car, everyone tried to hug
her at once.

"I'll come back this evening to give you a ride home,
sir," Mr. Smithens said to Uncle Hendrick.

Just before she went inside, Kit turned and waved

good-bye to Ruthie. "Thanks again! See you later!" she called. "Merry Christmas!"

"Merry Christmas!" Ruthie called back cheerily, waving through the car window.

❊

A merry Christmas it was, too, as merry as any Kit had ever known. Dad surprised Kit with her type-writer, fixed and as good as new, and Charlie gave her a box of typing paper. In the typewriter, there was a piece of paper that said:

```
Fur Kit, Morry Chri tma !
with luvo frum Dad and Charlio??
For Kit, Merry Christmas!
with love from Dad and Charlie
```

Mother had a surprise for Kit, too. It was a little black Scottie dog pin. "It was given to me when I was your age," said Mother with a twinkle in her eye. "I thought you might like it. Now that Uncle Hendrick is feeling better, you won't be seeing Inky quite so often."

At the sound of his name, Inky started barking. Kit

grinned at Mother. "Thanks, Mother," she said, over Inky's ruckus.

But the best surprise by far was Kit's surprise. Kit waited until she and Mother were alone in the kitchen mixing up a batch of waffles.

"We'll eat next to the tree," said Mother. She smiled a small smile. "I'm sure it'll be as lovely as ever, though I *am* sorry we can't have any lights on the tree this year. It just seemed too extravagant, since we can't pay the electric bill."

"Oh yes we can!" said Kit happily. She handed Mother a handkerchief full of coins. "Here's two dollars and forty cents."

Mother looked at the money in disbelief. "For heaven's sake!" she said. "Where did this come from, Kit?"

"From Uncle Hendrick," said Kit. "I earned it."

Mother laughed aloud. "Kit Kittredge," she said. "There never was a girl like you! Wait till I tell your father. He'll be just as proud of you as I am." She threw her arms around Kit and hugged her close. "I hope you are proud of yourself, too."

Kit was.

❄

At dusk, Ruthie and her father came back. Kit and Ruthie presented the scarves they had knitted to their fathers, who didn't seem to mind that the scarves had no fringe. Then Mr. Smithens drove Uncle Hendrick and Inky home, and Kit walked Ruthie back to her house.

They were quiet for a little while. Then Kit said, almost shyly, "Uncle Hendrick is all better. Would you . . . would you like to go window-shopping tomorrow?"

"Sure!" said Ruthie.

"The little Scottie pin my mother gave me will look really nice on the collar of your red dress," said Kit. "That is, if you don't mind if I borrow it." It was too dark to see Ruthie's face, but Kit could tell that she was smiling. Kit went on to say, "That was awfully nice of you to give the ballet tickets to Miss Hart and her boyfriend and Miss Finney and Mr. Peck."

"We can write about their romantic date in our newspaper," said Ruthie, "now that your dad fixed your typewriter. I bet you'll be glad to be writing again.

I bet you missed it while you were at your uncle's."

"Well . . ." said Kit. She hesitated, then she said, "Ruthie, I have sort of a present for you. It isn't store-bought or anything. But I made it for you. I hope you like it." Kit pulled a thick envelope out of her coat pocket and handed it to Ruthie. "Merry Christmas," she said.

Ruthie opened the envelope and took out Stirling's sketchpad. "The Story of Princess Ruthie," she read aloud from the cover. She looked through the pages. Kit had written a story to go with Stirling's sketches of Ruthie as a princess. "Oh, Kit!" said Ruthie. "Thank you! I know I'll love it. No one ever wrote a book for me before. And one about a princess, too!"

"She's a generous princess," said Kit. "Just like you. In fact, she *is* you. I was thinking of you the whole time I was writing about her."

"This is kind of funny," said Ruthie. "Wait till you see the present my mom and I made for you." Ruthie took a small package wrapped in tissue paper out of *her* coat pocket and handed it to Kit.

Kit unwrapped it and grinned from ear to ear. Ruthie had given her a doll that looked just like Amelia

Earhart! The doll was dressed in a flight cap and jacket and gloves just like the ones Amelia Earhart had worn in the newsreel, and she had the same good-humored, eager smile, too. "Thanks, Ruthie," Kit said. "This is the nicest present you could possibly have given me. You're a good friend."

"You're a good friend, too," said Ruthie. "I can't wait to read my princess story. See you tomorrow!"

"Bye," said Kit. "Merry Christmas!"

Kit watched Ruthie run up the driveway and go into the house. Then she turned around to walk home. When she saw her own house down the street, she gasped in surprise.

"Oh, how *beautiful*," she whispered. While she'd been walking Ruthie home, Dad and Charlie had put the lights on the Christmas tree. The lights were lit, and through the window, they glowed as brightly as jewels. Kit stood in the cold and stared at her family's house, where every happy Christmas of her life had taken place. *This may be the last Christmas we'll have in our house,* she thought, feeling a bittersweet joy. *But it's one I'll never forget. It may even have been the very best Christmas of all.*

INSIDE Kit's World

When Kit's father closed his business, the Kittredges
found themselves facing hard times that were shared
by millions of Americans. In 1929, America fell into a
financial crisis so serious that it came to be known as
the Great Depression. There had been depressions in
America's past, but none was as sudden, widespread,
and long-lasting as the Great Depression.

It began on October 29, 1929, a day that became
known as Black Tuesday. On that day, the stock market
"crashed" when stock prices dropped dramatically.
Many investors lost everything. They could not pay back
the money they had borrowed to buy stocks. The banks
that had loaned them money lost everything, too. Within
weeks, businesses and banks shut down all over the
country, and many thousands of people lost their jobs.

Almost overnight, families who had been comfortable found themselves with nothing. When a bank
closed, people were sometimes left with only the money
they had at home. Many people had nowhere to turn for
help and were deeply ashamed to go "on relief" or to
accept free meals in soup kitchens run by charities. For
most, it was the first time they had to rely on charity.
But with so many people in need, the charities soon ran
out of money, too. Families and neighbors helped one
another as much as they could, but often there was not
enough to go around.

People found creative ways to cope with the hard times. They planted gardens and raised animals for food, recycled everything they could, and made things they couldn't afford to buy. To save money, many families moved in together. Others turned their homes into boardinghouses, as Kit's family did.

Like the Kittredges, some families did all right during the first few years of the Depression, but few escaped the hard times entirely. Many children suffered. One West Virginia teacher noticed a student having trouble paying attention during class. When the girl didn't eat at lunchtime, the teacher suggested that the girl run home to get her lunch. She couldn't, the girl replied, because it was Tuesday—her sister's day to eat.

During the Depression, people looked for ways to forget their troubles. Many homes had radios, and families gathered to listen to the adventures of Little Orphan Annie and Buck Rogers or to the comedy team of George Burns and Gracie Allen.

The year 1932, when Kit's story begins, was the lowest point of the Great Depression. Unemployment was at an all-time high, and the future looked bleak. In November, Franklin Delano Roosevelt would be elected president, beating President Herbert Hoover by a landslide. Americans were desperate for a change, and they hoped that the new president would lead them out of the Depression.

Read more of KIT'S stories,
available from booksellers and at *americangirl.com*

❀ *Classics* ❀
Kit's classic series, now in two volumes:

Volume 1:
Read All About It!
Kit has a nose for news.
When the Great Depression
hits home, Kit's newsletters
begin making a real impact.

Volume 2:
Turning Things Around
With Dad still out of work,
Kit wonders if things will ever
get better. Could a letter to the
newspaper make a difference?

❀ *Journey in Time* ❀
Travel back in time—and spend a day with Kit!

Full Speed Ahead
Help Kit outwit Uncle Hendrick, find a missing puppy, and stay
out of jail when she's caught riding a freight train like a hobo! You
get to choose your own path through this multiple-ending story.

❀ *Mysteries* ❀
More thrilling adventures with Kit!

Intruders at Rivermead Manor
What's really going on in the old mansion next door?

Missing Grace
Kit's beloved basset hound has disappeared without a trace.

A Thief in the Theater
Can Kit catch the thief before the theater closes its doors for good?

Danger at the Zoo
With her reporter's instinct, Kit sniffs out some monkey business!

❋ A Sneak Peek at ❋

Turning Things Around

A Kit Classic
Volume 2

Kit's adventures continue in the
second volume of her classic stories.

s she and Stirling walked home, Kit felt tired and disheartened. A drop of rain dripped off the end of her nose. Kit swiped it with her hand, which was also wet. Everything was miserable and discouraging because of the leaden sky and dreary rain. Then, on the sidewalk ahead, Kit saw a muddy brown lump. She stopped.

"What is it?" asked Stirling.

Kit knelt down next to the lump. "It's a dog," she said, gently touching one wet, furry ear. "A poor, starving, pitiful dog." Attached to a string around the dog's neck was a soggy piece of paper with a message on it. The rain had blurred the writing so that the words had inky tears dripping from them, but Kit could read: *Can't feed her anymore.*

The dog sighed, and looked at Kit with the saddest eyes she'd ever seen. The look went straight to Kit's heart, making her forget all about her own hurt feelings. "Stirling, this dog's been abandoned," she said. "We've got to bring her home and feed her."

Stirling didn't hesitate. "Let's put her in the wagon," he said. "Aunt Millie will know how to save her."

"Come on, old girl," Kit said softly as she and Stirling awkwardly lifted the dog into the wagon. The poor creature looked like a bag of bones and fur with its short hind legs folded beneath its stomach, its long, forlorn face resting on its muddy front paws, and its droopy ears puddled around its head. The dog did not move or whimper the whole time Kit pulled the wagon home. It did not even lift its head when Kit stopped outside the screen door.

Stirling went into the kitchen and brought Aunt Millie outside.

"You've got to help, Aunt Millie," said Kit. "We think she's starving."

"Heavenly day!" said Aunt Millie. She bent down to examine the dog. "You children did the right thing, rescuing this poor dog. She's a sorrowful sight now, and I don't suppose she'll ever be a beauty, but she's a fine old hound. Not a thing wrong with her that food and loving care won't cure. She'll be a good guard dog for us and will more than earn her keep." Aunt Millie stood up and said briskly, "Put her in the garage. Keep her there until your mother's party is over. I'll rustle up some scraps and bring them out to you as soon as I can. Later, we'll bathe her."

As Kit and Stirling pulled the wagon to the garage, several things happened at once. The rain stopped, the clouds parted, and the sun shone at last. Mother and the garden club ladies came outside. They stood on the terrace to admire the azaleas, which looked heavenly with the raindrops sparkling on their delicate, colorful petals. The chickens were drawn outside by the sunshine, too. They emerged from their coop, strutting and clucking with enthusiasm, to peck in the mud for worms brought up by the rain.

At the sound of the chickens, the dog suddenly lifted its nose and sniffed the air. To Kit and Stirling's astonishment, the dog threw back its head and let loose a bloodcurdling howl. The ladies screeched, the chickens squawked, and the dog bolted out of the wagon and took off toward the chickens like a shot, barking wildly. Its lope was ungainly and awkward, but it was amazingly fast. Before anyone knew what was happening, the dog had chased some of the chickens across the lawn and onto the terrace, right into the middle of the ladies! The ladies protested as loudly as the chickens as the dog herded them all into the dining room, closely followed by Kit and Stirling.

Feathers flew. Kit chased the chickens and the dog around the tea table, trying to call to the dog above the ladies' shrieks. Dad, Charlie, and some of the boarders thundered down the stairs shouting, "What's going on?" Aunt Millie heard the racket and barreled out of the kitchen, flapping her apron at the chickens and shouting instructions to Kit.

Finally, Kit took a flying leap and tackled the dog. In so doing, she jostled the table. The china rattled like chattering teeth. The centerpiece of flowers rocked wildly. The candleholder tottered, fell over, then crashed to the floor. Somehow, Aunt Millie and Stirling shooed the chickens, who were still clucking indignantly, outside. Kit dragged the dog into the kitchen. She didn't dare take it outside until the chickens were safely shut up in their coop.

The calamity was over, but the party was ruined. The ladies scooped up their gloves and purses, said hurried thank-yous and good-byes to Mother, and scurried home. The house was suddenly quiet.

"I'm so sorry," said Kit when Mother came into the kitchen.

"You should apologize to Miss Mildred," said Mother wearily. "She's the one who worked so hard to make the party beautiful." Mother shook her head. "For myself, I don't know whether to laugh or cry. I've never seen such a disaster in all my life. Where on earth did that filthy dog come from?"

❉

About the Author

VALERIE TRIPP says that she became a writer because of the kind of person she is. She says she's curious, and writing requires you to be interested in everything. Talking is her favorite sport, and writing is a way of talking on paper. She's a daydreamer, which helps her come up with her ideas. And she loves words. She even loves the struggle to come up with just the right words as she writes and rewrites. Ms. Tripp lives in Maryland with her husband.